"No One Could Want To Leave This Place More Than I Do!"

Belinda said vehemently. "There are no happy memories here for me!"

"No one forced you to marry my father," Faron snarled. "You made your own bed. Now you have to lie in it. Just don't expect me to join you there."

Belinda's face blanched. She could feel his fury, his hate and his desire.

He took another step toward her.

"I'm warning you—"

Then it was too late. He had her in his arms before she could turn and run.

"Let me go!" she cried breathlessly. "This is wrong!"

"It's a little late for that argument, don't you think, Princess?"

"I didn't know who you were! I would never have..."

"Never have rolled in the grass with your stepson?"

Dear Reader,

Welcome to the merry month of May, where things here at Silhouette Desire get pretty perky. Needless to say, I think May's lineup of sexy heroes and spunky heroines is just fabulous... beginning with our star hunk, *Man of the Month* Cooper Maitland, in Jennifer Greene's *Quicksand*. This is one man you won't want to let get away!

Next, we have the second in Joan Johnston's HAWK'S WAY series, *The Cowboy and the Princess*. Now, please don't worry if you didn't read Book One, all of the HAWK'S WAY stories stand alone as great romantic reads.

Then the ever-popular Mary Lynn Baxter returns with *Mike's Baby* and Cait London appears with *Maybe No, Maybe Yes*. Maybe *you* won't want to miss *either* of these books! And don't pass up *Devil or Angel* by Audra Adams—just which best describes the hero, well, *I'm* not telling. Next, Carla Cassidy makes her Silhouette Desire debut with *A Fleeting Moment*. You'll never forget this witty, wonderful love story.

Yes, May is merry and filled with mayhem, but more important, it's filled with romance... only from Silhouette Desire. So, enjoy!

All the best,

Lucia Macro
Senior Editor

JOAN JOHNSTON
THE COWBOY AND
THE PRINCESS

SILHOUETTE *Desire*®

Published by Silhouette Books New York

America's Publisher of Contemporary Romance

SILHOUETTE BOOKS
300 East 42nd St., New York, N.Y. 10017

THE COWBOY AND THE PRINCESS

Copyright © 1993 by Joan Mertens Johnston

ISBN: 0-373-05785-7

First Silhouette Books printing May 1993

Printed in the U.S.A.

JOAN JOHNSTON

started reading romances to escape the stress of being an attorney with a major national law firm. She soon discovered that writing romances was a lot more fun than writing legal bond indentures. Since then, she has published a number of historical and contemporary category romances. In addition to being an author, Joan is the mother of two children. In her spare time, she enjoys sailing, horseback riding and camping.

One

He was a man who loved women. Blond or brunette, freckled or dimpled, witty or shy, Faron Whitelaw made it his business to discover the facet of each woman that made her uniquely beautiful. Needless to say, women found Faron irresistible. Even if he hadn't been handsome, which he was, they would have loved him for the innate thoughtfulness that always made him give as much as he took. Any woman who passed through Faron Whitelaw's life—whether in bed or out—received a gift that would remain with her a lifetime: the knowledge that she was a very special, desirable human being.

In fact, Faron had never known a woman he didn't like. Until now. At the age of thirty he had finally encountered the exception to the rule. He not only didn't like Belinda Prescott, he was prepared to hate her with a passion. Because, despite the fact he had never laid eyes on her, the woman was personally responsible for turning his life upside down.

"Want some company?"

Faron looked up at his eldest brother from the chair where he sat slouched with a whiskey in his hand. "Not particularly."

Garth snorted. "Too damn bad." He poured himself two fingers of whiskey and took the chair opposite Faron's in front of the stone fireplace. He put his feet up on a sturdy rawhide-covered stool that had held generations of Whitelaw boots. "I can't believe you're making so much out of this."

Faron's gray green eyes narrowed. His lips twisted into a bitter smile. "You're not the one who just found out he's a bastard."

Garth laughed. "Hell. I've been called a bastard all my life."

"That's how you act. It's what I *am*."

Faron's voice was stark as he asked, "How could Mom have done such a thing? Having an affair with some rich sonofabitch.... Did Dad know?"

Garth's lips flattened. "He knew." He paused and added, "So did I."

Faron stared into his brother's dark eyes, stunned by the realization that Garth had lived for years with this awful knowledge. "How long have you known that I was only half your kin?"

Garth looked away into the fire before he answered. "Since you were born."

"And you treated me like a real brother?"

"You *are* my brother!" Garth snapped. "Nothing's going to change that. Dad's name is on your birth certificate. He raised you. Nothing else matters."

Faron sneered. "You haven't read any of those letters from the widow—my stepmother—asking when I'm coming to claim my inheritance from my *father.*"

"Forget it," Garth advised. "There's plenty of Hawk's Way for both of us. You can stay right here in Texas, and we'll keep on raising and training quarter horses, just like we always have."

Faron shook his head. "I've got a mind to meet Belinda Prescott. The lawyer said she was the one who talked my fa—Wayne Prescott into putting me in his will. Said she *insisted* I get half of everything. Otherwise, I might never have known what Mom . . ." Faron's voice trailed off as his throat tightened up on him.

He had been feeling too much since he had found out that his beautiful mother had indulged in a tawdry affair with a millionaire rancher visiting Texas from Wyoming and had borne a bastard son.

It was a stunning revelation to Faron that he was only related *on his mother's side* to his older brothers Garth and Jesse and to his younger sister Tate. He felt bereft, wrenched from the bosom of his family. An outsider. And it was all that Prescott bitch's fault.

"I never figured the money would mean so much to you," Garth said in a quiet voice.

Faron's gray green eyes turned cold. "It's a good thing I grew up knowing how distrustful you are of everybody's motives. Otherwise I'd have to stand you up and knock you down for saying that. I'd have given anything not to know the truth. I don't want half that old man's fortune. I just want things to be the way they were."

The way they never would be again.

Garth swallowed half his glass of whiskey. But he didn't apologize. Faron hadn't expected him to. He began to understand a little better what had made Garth so cynical about women, why his older brother refused to trust the species, let alone love one of them. Faron might have felt the same way himself, if he had grown up knowing his mother had betrayed his father.

Both his parents were dead now. His mother had died giving birth to his sister, Tate, when Faron was seven. His father had broken his neck coming off an ornery bronc when Faron was fifteen. He felt ill equipped to deal with this secret that had been kept from him for so many years.

Faron tried to remember if his father—or mother—had treated him any differently than Garth or Jesse or Tate. But it was too painful to even think about that right now. He was still too shocked. And angry. And frustrated. He felt battered and needed to escape.

Faron played with the frayed seam at the knee of his jeans. "I just want to see the place where my fa— Where *he* came from," Faron said. "I can't explain it except to say that I feel like there's a hole inside me now that needs filling. Maybe I'll find something in Wyoming that'll give me the answers I need."

"Give my regards to Belinda Prescott," Garth said with a caustic smile.

"Your greetings will have to wait," Faron said grimly. "I've got a few things to say to Mrs. Prescott myself."

Belinda Prescott felt guilty as sin. She should be in mourning. Her husband of eight years had been buried a mere four months ago. She should be home wearing black and recounting the memories of her too-brief marriage. Instead she was riding the fastest horse in the stables across Wayne's Wyoming ranch, King's Castle, enjoying the early spring sunshine and feeling finally, at long last, *free*. Because for six of the past eight years, The Castle had been a prison and Wayne her jailer.

It hadn't started out that way, of course. She had met Wayne when she was a waitress in a short-order diner in Casper that he frequented. She had worked the graveyard shift trying to make ends meet, and he had often come in for a midnight breakfast. They had started talking, and one thing had led to another.

Wayne had found out that she was supporting three sisters. He was more than willing to accept a beautiful and youthful bride in exchange for a substantial trust fund for each of her siblings. She and Wayne had each known exactly what they were getting into. Twenty-year-old Belinda had willingly said her wedding vows with a man old enough to be her father. It was a small enough sacrifice to make so her sisters could have better lives.

She had been too young and desperate at the time to realize the ramifications of selling herself—body and soul—for money. In the years since, she had regretted her devil's bargain, but never so much as now, when she was finally free of Wayne and ready to go on with her life. Belinda had given up something besides her youth to marry Wayne—she had lost her innocence. She was no longer credulous, gullible or naive. She would never trust another man. The lessons Wayne had taught were hard, and he had been brutally thorough.

She spurred the mare beneath her into a lope and lifted her face to the sun. She didn't want to remember. But she couldn't forget.

Wayne had been such a gentle husband. At first. Then his heart had started causing him trouble. He had needed to take medication to keep him alive, and the medication had made him impotent. He had felt less a man and had sought other ways to relieve his frustration. He had begun to gamble. Then he drank to forget his huge gambling losses.

Slowly but surely he had become less gentle and more unreasonable in his demands. His fortune had dwindled until all that was left was The Castle, the land and a few prime head of breeding stock. And a twenty-eight-year-old wife who had learned that sometimes the price of security comes too high.

Belinda pulled the mare to an abrupt stop and wiped tears from eyes that were too blurred to see the grassy prairie around her. Her chest felt leaden—not because of sorrow, but because she felt none. God help her, she had felt only relief when the heart attack killed Wayne. It was difficult for her to look Wayne's mother, Madelyn, in the eye. Because Madelyn truly grieved, and Belinda could not.

At least she had been able to do one good thing. She had convinced Wayne to leave half of everything to his son. If it hadn't been for Wayne's mother, Belinda would have urged Wayne to leave his entire ranching empire to Faron Whitelaw. But Belinda had no money of her own. She hadn't had any trust fund put in her own name when she had married Wayne. He had gambled nearly everything else away. She had to have some way to take care of Madelyn, who had become as precious to her as her own mother.

Over the years, as Wayne had become more cruel, Madelyn had often stepped in to act as a buffer between her son and his wife. Madelyn had been appalled when she caught Wayne slapping Belinda. She had threatened to call the police if her son ever threatened Belinda with violence again. The two women had never spoken about Wayne, but they had shared other confidences, other hopes and dreams. Which was why Belinda had been determined to light a fire under her stepson that would goad him into moving north as soon as possible.

Belinda wondered what Faron Whitelaw would do when he learned the other conditions of Wayne's will. Her brow furrowed in concern. She had to hope that he would want his half of King's Castle enough to do what had to be done. She was counting on it. She was willing to do her part. She only hoped he would be willing to hang around long enough after he showed up to do his.

Otherwise they were both going to lose everything.

Two

Faron spoke softly as he unloaded the quarter horse gelding from the trailer. He had pulled his pickup well off the highway near a pasture gate. "I know it's been a long trip, Sonny. We're both tired of traveling. Just take it easy, boy. According to that old man at the gas station in Casper we're standing on Wayne Prescott's land. Just be patient a few more minutes until I get you saddled up, and we'll take ourselves a look-see."

The horse nickered as though he understood Faron and stood patiently while Faron brushed him down and saddled him up. It had been a long drive from northwest Texas to northeastern Wyoming.

As Faron stepped into the saddle he thought of what the white-haired gent at the gas station had told him about his father's land.

"Mr. Prescott had him a kingdom, all right. Called his spread King's Castle. Miles and miles of the prettiest grassland you ever did see," the old man had said. "That big old house is set off in the middle of nowhere. Near three stories high, made of gray stone, with them little pointy things on the roof like some storybook castle. Even called it The Castle, Mr. Prescott did."

Now, as Faron surveyed his father's domain, he was humbled by its vastness, awed by its richness. On this warm, surprisingly summerlike day in May, blue grama grass and wheatgrass flowed in waves over the rolling hills as far as the eye could see. This was cattle country, but there was a wealth of riches under the ground, as well. Oil. Natural gas. And coal.

Faron gave the horse his head and let him run. He felt the power of the animal beneath him, taking him farther into an untamed wilderness. He urged the animal on, as though by running faster he could escape the oppressive feelings that had haunted him since he had learned the truth about his birth.

It had taken him a week to put his things together after he had told Garth he was leaving. He had received yet another letter from Belinda Prescott asking him whether he was coming. She had sounded desperate. It made him wonder why she was so anxious for him to visit King's Castle. He had unbent enough to tell her he was coming, but he hadn't given her a definite date. His wire had simply said, "I'll be there when I get there."

Faron rode some distance from the highway, until there was nothing to remind him of the civilized world he had left behind. He couldn't believe his eyes when he spied a blond woman riding a palomino in the distance. Horse and rider presented a stunning picture. Her waist-length hair, flying like a gonfalon behind her, was the same magnificent gold as the horse's mane and tail.

He shouted to attract her attention. When she turned her head to stare at him, Faron drew breath with an audible gasp. She was incredibly beautiful. Ethereal. Like some fairy princess. He wondered for a moment if he had conjured her in his imagination.

But the shock on her face was real. And the sound of the palomino's thundering hooves as she galloped her horse away was real.

Intrigued, Faron pursued his elusive golden princess. He dug his heels in and urged his mount to a run. The quarter horse was bred for speed over short distances, and Faron quickly overtook the woman. He grabbed the palomino's bridle and hauled her horse to a stop.

The woman stared at him wide-eyed, wary.

Faron smiled. It was a smile that said, "You can trust me. I won't hurt you. I find you absolutely lovely."

But his elusive princess—who else but a princess would he find on King's Castle land?—wasn't the least bit impressed.

"Let me go," she said in a breathless voice. "Please."

He let go of the bridle but said, "Don't go. Stay and talk with me."

She took her lower lip between her teeth. He could see her distress, the struggle to decide. "We're strangers," she said at last. "We have nothing to talk about."

"If we talk, we won't be strangers for long," he promised. "Please."

"I have to go home."

"What's your name?" he asked.

"None of your business."

"All right, then. No names. I'll call you Princess. You can call me . . . Cowboy."

He thought he saw the hint of a smile curl her lip, but she flattened it out damn quick. Faron stepped down from his horse and walked around its head to stand at her side. He tipped his Stetson back and smiled up at her. "I'll help you down."

He didn't give her a chance to object. Before she could say anything Faron had got hold of her tiny waist. He could feel the tension in her as he lifted her off the horse. She met his gaze for an instant with frightened eyes before she lowered her lashes, and he realized that she expected him to take advantage of the situation. Maybe he should have dragged her down the length of him. He sure as hell had wanted to bad enough.

She clearly had a body made for loving. She was nearly as tall as he was. Her head came all the way to his chin, which was surprising because he was well over six feet. She was wearing a long-sleeved man's shirt tucked into fitted Levi's, but both shirt and jeans showed off a figure that was fully feminine. Her boots were well used but expensive, ostrich if he wasn't mistaken.

He had to bite the inside of his cheek to keep from gasping when she glanced up at him again. She had eyes a rare violet color. Her complexion would have earned the envy of a pale pink rose. As he stared at her, stricken by emotions he couldn't name, he saw her cheeks darken to a redder rose.

"I should go home," she said. But she sounded less sure about leaving. She was worrying that full lower lip again with pearly white teeth.

Faron slipped her hand through his crooked arm, took the reins of both horses and started walking toward a meadow of spring wildflowers. "It's a beautiful day, isn't it, Princess?"

He could feel the tension in her, and he kept talking in an attempt to show her he wasn't a threat to her. At least not yet.

"Tell me about yourself," he urged.

She eyed him from beneath lowered lashes. "What do you want to know?"

"Any brothers or sisters?"

For the first time, her lips curved in a genuine smile. Sweet and kind of sad. "Three sisters."

"Older or younger?"

"All younger. You?"

Faron opened his mouth to say two brothers and a sister, then realized he would have to qualify that—half-brothers and a half-sister. He frowned. Damned if he would. "I've got two older brothers and a younger sister."

He felt her relax almost immediately. Amazing how having a family made him seem less dangerous. Little did she know. His family was about the most unruly bunch he knew. "What are you doing way out here?" he asked.

She looked off into the distance. "Running from my problems."

He was tempted to make a flippant retort, but her honesty spurred him to equal sincerity. "Me, too."

She looked up at him again from beneath those dark lashes, to see if he was telling the truth. He realized she hadn't once looked at him directly and figured she must be used to hiding her feelings. But from whom? And why?

His lips twisted wryly. "Seems like we do have something in common, Princess. How 'bout if we run off together and leave our problems behind?"

"I can't—"

"Just for the afternoon," he urged. "What do you say? Let's throw our cares to the four winds and enjoy this afternoon together."

He felt her hand tremble where it lay on his forearm. She withdrew it and clasped her hands together in front of her. He could see she was tempted. He wished he knew what to say to push her over the brink. Nothing came to mind, so he just smiled.

Belinda knew she was making a mistake even as she nodded her head yes. She had to be crazy. She was truly certifiable. Imagine agreeing to spend the afternoon with a perfect stranger. She recognized the quality of both his horse and saddle, so she knew he was more than just some drifter. He was wearing frayed jeans, but his Western shirt appeared to have been tailored to fit both his broad shoulders and his lean waist.

But who was he? And where had he come from? She had lived so reclusively at The Castle, he might even be a neighbor from one of the outlying spreads for all she knew. "Are you from around here?" she asked.

"Just passing through."

That was some comfort. "What brings you here?"

He looked off across the prairie. "Just taking a look around. How about you? You live around here?"

She nodded. "Around." She wasn't about to be any more specific than he had been. It was safer that way.

Apparently the Cowboy gave her evasive answer a different meaning because he grinned and said, "So you're trespassing, too?"

"What?"

"Trespassing. On Wayne Prescott's land."

"Oh." Belinda knew she ought to correct his mistaken impression, but that would mean admitting she was Wayne Prescott's widow. Which would mean an abrupt end to her afternoon with the Cowboy. She wanted—needed—to forget who she was for a little while. So she said nothing.

Faron took her revealing blush as an admission of equal guilt. He smiled and said, "Don't worry. I won't let you get into trouble." After all, he owned half the place. If that bitch stepmother of his tried to make trouble, well, he would handle her. He pulled off his worn leather gloves and tucked them in his belt. Then he held out his hand to her. "I feel like walking some more. Will you join me?"

His smile made the invitation irresistible. Belinda's heart was doing a *rat-a-tat-tat* that made her want to press her hands to her chest to slow it down. She forcibly relaxed the knotted fingers she had clasped in front of her and reached out to take his hand. It was warm and callused like a working man's ought to be. It gave her a feeling of strength and security as it closed around her fingers.

At the same time, she looked up into the Cowboy's unusual gray green eyes. They were the color of a mountain spruce, wide set, heavily lashed and crowned with arched brows. There were webbed lines at the corners, etched there by the sun. His nose was straight and angled slightly at the tip, and he had a beauty mark—was it called that when a man had one?—high on his right cheekbone.

She had been terrified when he chased her on horseback, but he had done a good job of allaying her fears. He hadn't touched her in any except the most gentlemanly way. She had noticed his restraint when he lifted her off her horse. On the other hand, he hadn't exactly given her a choice of whether she was going to join him on the ground. She felt certain he wasn't the sort of man to be denied something he wanted.

Nevertheless, she was inclined to accept him at face value. He was an open, friendly and—she would not deny it—handsome man...who knew his way around women. She had been charmed by that ridiculous name he had called her, Princess. And it was telling that he had tagged himself Cowboy, after that chivalrous knight of the Old West.

So what did he *really* want from her? She angled her head and took a long hard look at him.

"Something wrong?" he asked.

"You look familiar somehow."

He grinned. "Maybe I'm the man you've been waiting for all your life."

Her expression sobered. She was waiting for someone, all right, but it wasn't the man of her dreams. Any day now she expected her stepson from Texas to arrive. For a horrified instant she wondered if this stranger with whom she had been flirting could be Faron Whitelaw.

But this man couldn't be Wayne's son. He didn't look a bit like Wayne. Wayne's well-trimmed hair had been almost white blond. This man had coal black hair hanging down over his collar. Nor did his gray green eyes have anything in common with the cold sapphire of Wayne's. And the Cowboy's forearms, visible where his shirtsleeves were folded up, revealed a warm bronze tint totally different from Wayne's light, easily freckled skin.

Did it really matter who he was? Would it be so awful if she stole an afternoon for herself with a perfect stranger? She had seen the admiration in his eyes, and it felt good. She had found him equally attractive.

He was extraordinarily tall, which was a good thing, since she had been as long-legged as a giraffe all her life. He had the rangy build of a cowboy, long, lean and strong. He had lifted her from the saddle as though she weighed nothing. And she had felt the play of muscle and sinew where her hand rested on his forearm.

Why not join in the Cowboy's fantasy? Just for an afternoon. What could possibly go wrong?

"So what are you running from?" Belinda asked as she strolled with the Cowboy toward the nearby meadow.

Faron left the two horses with their reins dragging. A cow horse wouldn't wander far ground-tied like that, and there was plenty of grass to keep the animals close.

"I think this is only going to work if we leave our problems behind us," Faron said. "We can only talk about good things this afternoon." He stopped and turned to face her. "Agreed?"

"It's a deal," Belinda said.

He lifted the hand he held, turned it over and kissed the center of her palm.

Belinda felt a streak of electricity shoot up her arm. She yanked her hand back reflexively, then laughed to cover the awkwardness it had created between them. "That tickled," she murmured in excuse and explanation.

"Yeah," he muttered back. Faron wondered if she had felt the same charge on her skin as he had felt on his lips. It had been an amazingly strong jolt to his system.

"Let's sit down, shall we?" Belinda dropped to her knees near a patch of large, daisylike flowers. Nearby was a bunch of bright blue lupine. The top of the hillside was rimmed with Indian paintbrush.

"We couldn't have picked a more perfect spot for an afternoon idyll if we'd tried," she said.

Faron's eyes narrowed as he surveyed the countryside. "It is beautiful. It's a shame..."

"What?"

"Nothing." Faron wasn't about to spoil his afternoon by thinking about his father and stepmother. He sat down and realized the ground still held the chill of winter. He pulled off his denim jacket and said, "Why don't you sit on this? It'll keep you from getting cold."

"I don't think—"

Again, he didn't give her a choice. He spread his jacket on the ground, then slipped a hand around her waist and resettled her on the denim. "Thanks," she murmured.

Faron's gallantry won him a rare smile that made his heart skip a beat. "You're welcome."

Belinda immediately began making a chain from the daisylike flowers. Faron stretched out beside her, his head on his hand.

"God, you're beautiful," he said.

Belinda laughed. "Are you always so forthright?"

He felt his body tighten at the sound of her laughter. "I tend to say what I'm thinking."

She looked up at him from under lowered lashes. "Then since we're being honest, you're quite good-looking yourself."

He grinned. "Thanks."

She laughed again. He was so different from Wayne. So carefree. She ought not to be here. She ought to be home, wearing black. Mourning.

"What are you thinking, Princess?"

The Cowboy's voice ripped her from the melancholy that threatened her peace. "What?"

He smoothed the furrows on her brow with his thumb. She had to purposely hold herself still for the caress. It was the first one she had received in so long her skin seemed to come alive beneath his touch. When his fingers trailed into the hair at her temple she leaned away, and his hand dropped back to the grass.

"You looked worried," he said. "I wondered what you were thinking."

"That I shouldn't be here."

"No time for regrets now. We made a deal. Only happy thoughts." Faron sat up and leaned his wrist on one bent knee. "Let's see. What should we talk about?"

"When was the happiest time in your life?" she asked.

"It's all been pretty good," he admitted. Until lately. "I guess I'd choose the day I made love to a woman for the first time."

Faron was both surprised and delighted by the blush that stained her cheeks at his revelation.

"I can't believe you said that," Belinda protested with a laugh.

"I warned you I was honest," Faron said. "It's your turn now."

"The happiest time?" she asked. There was a long silence while she thought about it.

"It wasn't that tough a question, was it?" Faron asked.

She grimaced. "I suppose the happiest time would have been before my parents died, although life was such a struggle on the ranch..." She shrugged.

Belinda could see the Cowboy was about to ask questions she would rather not answer, so she asked, "What did you want to be when you grew up?"

"That's easy," Faron replied. "The best."

"At what?"

"Something. Anything."

"That certainly gave you a lot of room to succeed," she said teasingly. Apparently he hadn't liked the idea of being tied down to any one thing. "Are you the best at something?"

Faron grinned. "I'm a damned good cowboy, ma'am." He leaned back so she could see the rodeo belt buckle he was wearing.

Belinda laughed and realized suddenly it had been a long time since she had done so. "I should have known." She leaned over and traced the writing on the buckle with her fingertips. *Rodeo Cowboy All-Around Champion.*

No wonder he had called himself Cowboy!

Faron held his breath as Belinda traced the face of the silver buckle with her fingertips. It was as though he could actually feel her touching his skin. He wanted her hand lower. His body was doing a helluva good job of imagining all by itself.

He cleared his throat, distracting her attention. "How about you? What did you want to be?"

"I never let myself dream. I couldn't."

"Why not?"

She draped a chain of flowers around the brim of his Stetson. "My sisters and I were orphaned when my parents were killed in a car accident. I was eighteen and had just graduated high school. Dori and Tillie and Fiona were still in school. The ranch went to the bank for debts. I found a job in Casper that paid enough to feed us and keep a roof over our heads. That didn't leave much time for dreaming."

"Let's pretend you're a real princess, and you can have anything you want. What would you wish for?" Faron asked. He laid a handful of flowers he had broken off just below the bud in her lap.

She scooped up the white, yellow and blue flowers and lifted them to her nose to see how they smelled. "I'd wish for a man to love me. And for children. I've always wanted to have children."

"How many children?" he asked in a quiet voice.

"More than one," she said definitely. "I liked having sisters. I grew up knowing I never had to be alone."

"Do your sisters live close?"

"Unfortunately they're scattered across the country. Every Fourth of July we get together. That's the only time everyone can get free."

Which meant she spent the rest of the year alone, Faron deduced.

Her lashes fluttered down to conceal her eyes. "You're not wearing a ring. Are you married?"

"No."

"Do you have a girlfriend?"

"No."

"But you've had lots of them, I suspect."

Faron eyed her askance. "What makes you say that?"

"You're awfully charming, for one thing."

He shrugged. "If you say so."

She smiled. "I do. For another thing, you don't seem in any hurry to... Her cheeks felt warm. "I don't know exactly how to say this."

"Jump your bones?"

Her flush deepened. "Well, I wouldn't have said it quite that way, but—"

"The afternoon isn't over yet."

She swallowed hard. "Then I'm not safe with you?"

"As safe as you want to be," he said in a husky voice.

His eyes were more green than gray as they sought hers. Belinda was aware of a frisson of desire that began in her belly and spiraled upward.

She could feel herself being drawn to him. She had already begun to lean toward him when she realized what she was doing. She jumped abruptly to her feet, scattering flowers around her. "It's getting late. I have to go."

She had already started toward her horse when he caught up to her and grasped her arm, stopping her. "Are you sure you can't stay a little longer?"

Belinda looked at the sun lowering in the western sky. Why, several hours must have passed! Where had the time gone? The Cowboy had cast some sort of spell on her to make her forget who—and what—she was. She would be lucky to get back to The Castle before suppertime. Madelyn would worry if she wasn't home by then. "I have to leave. Really, this has been lovely, but I have to go."

"Where do you live? When can I see you again?"

"You can't!" She hadn't meant to be curt, but she couldn't bear to see the look in his eyes if he ever found out she was a widow, a woman who should be in mourning. "You can't," she said more calmly, but just as firmly.

"Why not?"

"Because . . . please don't ask me to explain."

"All right."

Belinda breathed a sigh of relief. It turned out to be premature.

"I'll settle for a goodbye kiss."

"What?"

He didn't give her a chance to argue about it, simply pulled her into his arms and captured her mouth with his.

The Cowboy's kiss was like nothing Belinda had ever experienced before in her life. He tunneled all ten fingers into her hair. His lips softened on hers, and his tongue slipped inside her mouth to tease and to taste. For a moment she was quiescent. Then she kissed him back.

Faron hadn't known what to expect when he kissed his Princess. He had supposed from her shyness that he would be tasting innocence. For a few moments he had. But she had pulled him down to a deeper, darker well of desire than he had ever explored with a woman. A well where feelings and emotions were intimately bound with the physical act of love.

He lifted his head far enough to look into her eyes. "Princess?"

Belinda gazed up into gray green orbs that were fierce with need. She reached up to touch the beauty mark on the Cowboy's cheek, then trailed her fingertips back down to his mouth, which was still wet from their kiss. She traced his lips with her forefinger, then looked up into eyes that had darkened with desire. She raised her mouth and touched it lightly to his. Then her tongue slipped inside his mouth to taste him.

She could feel the restraint he exercised to remain still for her kiss. It made her dare more. Her hands slipped around his neck and her fingertips teased the hair at his nape. She kissed the edges of his mouth and lingered to nip at his lower lip with her teeth. A harsh sound grated deep in the Cowboy's throat, and Belinda found herself answering with a kittenish purr of satisfaction.

He kissed his way along the edge of her jaw to her ear and caressed the delicate shell with his tongue. His breath was hot and moist and sent a shiver down her spine. Then his tongue slipped into her ear, and her belly curled with erotic sensation.

Belinda's eyes closed in surrender as her body swayed toward his. The Cowboy's arms closed around her, pulling her tight against him. She could feel the blunt ridge of his manhood against her femininity. As he rocked their bodies together, Belinda felt her knees give way.

The two of them slipped to the ground together. Belinda was aware of the cool grass beneath her, but it was the warmth above that she found so intriguing. The Cowboy held most of his weight on his arms, but their bodies were pressed together from the waist down, their legs entwined. His mouth found hers again, and this time he was more impatient.

One yank ripped the first three buttons on her shirt free. His mouth was reverent as he kissed the creamy mounds that spilled out of her lacy bra. He freed the bra itself, and his mouth latched on to a rosy crest. When he began to suck, Belinda's whole body arched up into his.

She was desperate to touch his skin, and she pulled at his shirt to free it from his jeans. She tried to unbutton the buttons, but her hands were trembling too much. The Cowboy ripped the shirt off himself, sending buttons flying. Then he pressed their bodies together, flesh to flesh. Belinda made a soft little sound in her throat as the crisp hair on his chest brushed her tender nipples.

"Princess, you feel so good. You feel so right." His hand slid down to unsnap her jeans. The rasp of her zipper coming down sounded loud in her ears. Before she could come to her senses his mouth had captured her breast again. The Cowboy sucked and nipped and sucked again so the sensual tension never let up.

His hand slid down inside her panties, through her feminine curls until he found the tender bud he sought. Belinda nearly came up off the ground as his fingers began to work their magic.

"Come apart for me, Princess," Faron crooned. "Be beautiful for me, only me."

He shoved her jeans down out of the way and unfastened his own. Belinda caught his face with both hands and brought his mouth up to hers.

"Kiss me, Cowboy. Please, kiss me."

She felt his body invade hers at the same time his tongue thrust into her mouth. He was big and hard, and her body arched up to take all of him as he thrust deeply inside her. Belinda heard an animal sound rip from her throat as their bodies surged together. He withdrew and thrust again in ageless rhythm as her hips rose in counterpoint to his.

Her fingernails dug crescents in his shoulders as her body arched up in passion. At the last instant, Belinda tried to fight the pleasure. This shouldn't be happening! She had no right!

But the Cowboy wouldn't allow her to withdraw. "Come with me, Princess. Come with me!"

Then it was too late. Her body began to convulse in wave after wave of unbearable pleasure. She gritted her teeth against the ecstasy that besieged her, holding her prisoner for timeless moments. While she was caught in the throes of passion, the Cowboy claimed her for his own. His cries were guttural as his body arched and spilled its seed within her.

Afterward, they both lay exhausted, unable to move. Belinda was aware of a fine sheen of sweat on his body and the musky smell of sex.

"I want to see you again," the Cowboy murmured as he slipped to her side and drew her into his arms. He was already asleep before Belinda could answer him.

Which was just as well.

Belinda was appalled at what she had done. But she couldn't regret it. What had passed between the Cowboy and his Princess was one brief shining moment when two souls blended into one. They might be strangers still, but they had found something more than physical satisfaction in each other's arms. She would hold this magical afternoon close to her heart forever.

But there was no way she could see him again. He would be horrified if he knew the truth about her. And she would be ashamed for him to find out. She had to escape now, while he was asleep.

She dressed quickly and quietly and led her palomino a short distance away before she mounted him, so that she wouldn't wake the Cowboy. When she was far enough away that the sound wouldn't waken him, she kicked the mare into a gallop and raced back to The Castle.

The instant she stepped inside the kitchen door, she was greeted by her mother-in-law. Belinda plowed a hand through her hair, shoving it off her face, and tried a smile. It failed dismally.

"You're late," Madelyn said. She took one look at Belinda's disheveled appearance and asked, "What happened to you?" There was more curiosity than accusation in her tone.

"I . . . my horse threw me," Belinda said, brushing at the grass stains on her jeans.

"Your blouse is ripped. Are you sure you're all right?"

Belinda flushed and clutched at the torn fabric. Getting thrown shouldn't have torn three buttons off her blouse. "I'll just run upstairs and change for supper." She hurried from the kitchen and practically ran up the majestic circular staircase that led to her bedroom.

"There's no hurry," Madelyn murmured to Belinda's disappearing back. There would be plenty of time before supper to ask about the love-bruise on her daughter-in-law's neck.

Three

The cool night air woke Faron. At first he didn't know where he was. It all came back to him in a hurry. As he dressed himself, one thing quickly became apparent. His Princess was gone.

Faron was furious when he realized he didn't know her name or how to find her. Nor could he track her in the dark. Besides, he had phoned The Castle from Casper, and Madelyn Prescott was expecting him for dinner.

He dressed quickly, muttering profanities when he realized half the buttons were gone from his shirt. He would have to change it when he got back to his truck. He took a look at the knees of his jeans and realized it probably wouldn't hurt to change them, either. Not that he gave a damn what the Prescotts thought of him, but he had been taught manners around ladies that were hard to shed.

Faron whistled for his horse, and Sonny nickered a response. The quarter horse hadn't drifted far. Faron mounted up and rode in the fading light of dusk back in the direction of his truck and trailer. There wasn't any chance he would lose his way. He had learned young to look back every so often when he was riding the range to mark his trail. He easily found the landmarks that took him back to the highway.

Faron had gotten directions from Madelyn Prescott, and it didn't take him long to find the formal entrance to King's Castle. If the land had awed him, the house itself—The Castle—left him speechless.

As he stepped from his pickup he couldn't help staring. Light poured from tall, narrow, leaded windows, and there were sconces on the outside stone walls that created an eerie silhouette on the plains. The house did indeed have crenels along the roofline and what appeared to be turrets at the corners.

When he cut the engine a cowhand came from the direction of the barn.

"I'm Toby, Mr. Whitelaw. Mrs. Prescott said I was to take care of your horse," the cowhand said.

Faron backed the horse from the trailer and watched long enough to make sure the cowhand knew what he was doing before he left his horse in Toby's care.

Moments later Faron found himself on the front steps of The Castle. The three-story gray stone structure had a massive double wooden door headed by a stone arch that might once have been the gateway to a medieval castle. When Faron knocked, the imposing entrance was opened by a tiny, silver-haired lady dressed in black. He found himself looking into a pair of gray green eyes the same unusual color as his own.

"Hello, Faron," the woman said with a smile of greeting, "I'm your grandmother, Madelyn Prescott. We've been expecting you."

Faron's hat came off at once. He leaned over and kissed the old woman on the cheek. She smelled of lavender powder. Her skin had the softness of the very young and the very old. The wrinkles on her face gave her character as well as age. Faron felt his throat tighten as he realized this woman was indeed his grandmother. It was true, then. He was a bastard.

Madelyn cupped her grandson's cheek with her hand and searched his features looking for signs of Wayne. There was nothing of her son in Faron, but there was something of her. "You've got the Halliwell eyes, I see."

"If you say so, ma'am," Faron said. "Hope I'm not too late for supper."

"Not at all. Belinda is still upstairs getting dressed. Perhaps you'd like to share a brandy with me in the parlor while we wait."

"I'd be pleased to, ma'am."

"Please, call me Madelyn."

But Faron couldn't bring himself to call his grandmother by her first name. It seemed disrespectful somehow. By what fond nickname would he have called her, he wondered, if he had known as a child that she existed? He had called his father's mother Nanaw, and his mother's mother Gram. "Would you mind if I called you Maddy?" he asked.

Her gray green eyes quickly misted, and she pressed a fragile hand against her heart. "Why, that would be lovely, Faron."

He frowned when she seemed to have trouble catching her breath. "Are you all right?"

"My health isn't what it used to be. My heart, you know."

"I didn't know. Have you seen a doctor?"

"Oh, yes. I'm afraid in my case it's just a matter of age catching up with me. Come along now. Belinda will be down soon, I'm sure."

As Faron followed Madelyn, he stepped into a world of days gone by—an open drawing room with walnut woodwork, nineteenth century furniture of polished cherry and oak, lace curtains and brilliant chandeliers of sparkling crystal. Two broad stairways formed a sweeping arc leading to the upper floors.

Faron frowned at what he saw only because it represented his father's wealth, which was the source of the current calamity in his life. It was not the setting in which he had expected to find his ogre of a stepmother. It felt too much like a home. He couldn't help but admire the sense of history that was represented in the antique Western furnishings.

Faron and his grandmother had gotten only as far as the stairs when they heard the echo of footsteps.

"That will be Belinda," Madelyn said.

Faron followed her gaze up the stairs. The composed, graceful young woman who came walking down the sweeping staircase was a far cry from the ugly stepmother found in fairy tales. In fact, she was his very own Princess.

Her glorious golden hair, which he had grasped in his fists while he came inside her mere hours ago, was bound up now in a stylish twist. Her sleek black silk dress showed off a lush figure with which he was intimately familiar. A long black chiffon scarf circled her neck and floated on the air behind her. But there was nothing of the wanton woman he had loved reflected in the cool violet eyes that met his gaze.

It would be difficult to say which of the two lovers was more shocked to see the other. It was equally apparent that neither of them was willing to do or say anything in front of Madelyn that would upset the old woman.

"Good evening, Mr. Whitelaw," Belinda said, extending her hand. Her heart was pounding, and she felt as though she were going to faint. When the Cowboy took her hand, he held it longer than he should. His mouth had formed into a smile, but his gray green eyes looked wintry.

"It's a pleasure to meet you at last, Mrs. Prescott. Please call me Faron. If you don't mind, I'll call you... Belinda."

Faron's anger had returned with a vengeance. Here stood a woman he had hated sight unseen— but with whom he had just experienced an incredibly passionate assignation. He wanted to ask her why she had made love to him when her husband—his father—was barely cold in the ground. But his lips clamped tight on the question. What they had done was awful enough. He had no intention of embarrassing his grandmother with revelations that would have to be distasteful to her.

Beyond being angry, Faron was hurt. His stepmother had made a fool of him. He had called The Castle from Casper hours ago, so she must have known he was coming. Which meant she also must have known who he was when she had made love with him. No wonder she hadn't wanted to give him her name! How could she have done such a thing?

But despite being angry and hurt, he was also aroused. The memory of what had happened between them was still fresh, like a green wound that ached when prodded. Even icily distant, she was still his Princess. And he wanted her as much now as he ever had.

Tension lay thick in the air. A powerful current sparked between them, threatening a shock to the first who broke it.

"Come along, children," Madelyn said at last. She led the way to the dining room, which was as richly furnished as the rest of the house. The pine trestle table was at least fifteen feet long. Three places had been set at one end with fine china and silver.

Faron held Madelyn's chair as she sat at the head of the table. Then he went around to help Belinda. Her stomach clenched when Faron leaned over to whisper in her ear and trailed his hand across her bare shoulder. When he spoke, it was his anger she heard.

"It didn't take you long to find some young stud to service you," he hissed. "Did I measure up to my father?"

Belinda's face bleached white.

"Are you feeling all right, my dear?" Madelyn asked.

"I'm a little tired," Belinda said. "I had a long ride this afternoon." She raised her eyes to meet Faron's and realized the second meaning that could be given to her words. His lips lifted in a slight smirk that made her feel physically ill.

Belinda wanted to tell him she was sorry. But she wasn't sorry. What had happened between them had been beautiful. What she really wanted was the chance to explain why she had needed what he had offered. She had been so very vulnerable. It had been so wonderful to allow herself the fantasy of loving and being loved.

Now Belinda was sure Faron Whitelaw had entirely the wrong idea about what kind of woman she was. She could feel his attraction to her, but it was laced with harsher, harder feelings. The fierce look on his face gave ample evidence that he didn't want to hear what she had to say. And that he was unlikely to forgive or forget what she had done.

When Belinda realized the road her thoughts had taken she was alarmed. Hadn't she learned her lesson with Wayne? Here she was ready to make the same mistakes again! Why should she care what her stepson thought of her? She would never give another man the sort of emotional, physical and economic hold over her that Wayne had possessed.

She ought to show Faron the door. If it had only been herself involved in the catastrophe that threatened, she would have. But there was Madelyn to think of. So she clamped her back teeth together and held her tongue.

Once Faron was seated, an older woman wearing a voluminous white apron began serving dinner. She passed out plates already laden with pork chops, mashed potatoes and green beans. The servant had hair dyed a shocking red and fingernails painted an equally vivid color. When she left the room Madelyn said, "Rue has been with the family forever. Belinda and I couldn't manage without her."

To Faron it was further proof that Belinda Prescott was the pampered Princess he had labeled her. His stepmother sat across from him looking cool and elegant and totally in control. Meanwhile, his body was hard and throbbing from the small caress of her shoulders he had allowed himself. But he would be damned if he'd touch her again anytime soon.

As he ate his dinner, Faron tried to revive the feelings of dislike he had felt toward Belinda Prescott for forcing him to confront his true paternity. But it was one thing to hate a woman you envisioned as an interfering Rich Bitch, and quite another to hate a woman with whom you've just shared the most poignant physical encounter of your life.

To compound his confusion, the woman he found so attractive was his stepmother. He had been determined not to take anything handed down to him from Wayne Prescott. Now he found there was one thing he wanted very much: his father's widow.

"Did Belinda write you about the terms of the will?"

Madelyn's question jerked Faron from his thoughts. "What?"

"The will. Did Belinda tell you the terms of Wayne's will?"

Faron's gaze swung back around the table to spear Belinda. "No, Maddy, she didn't. She did seem in an all-fired hurry for me to get here."

"Why don't you tell Faron the problem, Belinda," Madelyn said.

"If you came here expecting to inherit wealth beyond your dreams, you're going to be disappointed," Belinda began.

Faron's brows arched. "I heard my father was a millionaire."

"*Was* is the correct word," Belinda said. "King's Castle, including the land and The Castle on it, is mortgaged to the hilt. The mineral leases only provide enough income to cover the taxes, and the worsening economy has left the ranch only marginally profitable."

"So sell the ranch and move into town," Faron said.

"It isn't that simple."

"Why not?" Faron asked.

"If we could sell the property piecemeal, there might be some hope of making a profit and avoiding foreclosure. But Wayne's will stipulates that King's Castle has to be sold all in one piece. Otherwise it gets donated to charity.

"We simply haven't been able to find a buyer willing to take the whole thing—thousands of acres of land, dozens of buildings, farm equipment, the stock, the house—in short, someone willing to buy the losing aspects of the ranch along with the profitable ones," Belinda explained. "I was hoping you might have some ideas about improvements that would make the ranch attractive to a single corporate buyer."

Faron had wondered why his stepmother had gone to so much trouble to have him included in his father's will. Now he had his answer. She needed someone with the right motivation—a promise of half the proceeds—to spend the time and energy putting King's Castle back on its feet so she could make a big killing when it was sold!

His sense of self-preservation warned him to get right back in his truck and go home to Texas. He decided to ask a few more questions first.

"How much money do you have to work with?"

"You mean cash?" Belinda asked. When Faron nodded she said, "There's just enough in the bank for food for us and the stock over the summer."

"Surely there are some jewels or furs you can liquidate," Faron said.

"Oh, dear, no," Madelyn said. "Wayne sold all those things years ago."

"Have you tried cutting the staff for the house and the number of cowboys on the payroll."

Madelyn's eyes twinkled as she laughed. "You've seen the house staff," she said.

"Rue?" Faron asked incredulously.

"We simply couldn't let her go," Madelyn said. "She's almost family."

"And the cowhands?"

"You've met Toby, I presume."

Faron nodded. When Madelyn said nothing more he realized the middle-aged cowboy was all there was. "Who takes care of things around here?" he demanded.

"Why, Belinda does, of course," Madelyn said.

Faron stared hard at his stepmother. That wasn't at all what he had expected to hear.

"I can see you two need to discuss business," Madelyn said. "So I'll just excuse myself and go upstairs and get some rest."

Faron stood and escorted his grandmother to the door of the dining room, sliding the wooden door closed behind her. Then he turned back to the woman who had become his nemesis—and his desire.

Faron stared at Belinda with narrowed eyes. "How bad is it?" he demanded.

She laced her hands together calmly. "It's as bad as you think it is. We're as poor as church mice. If something isn't done to make King's Castle salable, Madelyn and I will be penniless and homeless within the year."

Faron fisted his hands so hard his knuckles turned white. He might have been able to leave Belinda to her fate, but there was no way he could stand by and watch his own grandmother be put out in the street.

"All right," he said. "I'll hang around long enough to help put the place in shape to sell. But as soon as we find a buyer, I'm out of here!"

"No one could want to leave this place more than I do!" Belinda said vehemently. "There are no happy memories here for me!"

"No one forced you to marry my father," Faron snarled. "You made your own bed. Now you have to lie in it. Just don't expect me to join you there."

Belinda's face blanched white. She could feel his fury, his hate and his desire. She had learned from Wayne how to avoid confrontation. It didn't always work, but often enough it had saved her a bruise or a blackened eye. She put those lessons to good use now.

She lowered her eyelids to hide the anger blazing there. She rose and smoothed the front of her skirt with hands that appeared much more calm than they were. In a soft, deferential voice she said, "I believe I'll retire now."

When Faron took a step toward Belinda, her eyes flashed defiance. She would not become a victim, ever again. "Keep your distance, Cowboy!"

He took another step toward her.

"I'm warning you—"

Then it was too late. He had her in his arms before she could turn and run.

"Let me go," she cried breathlessly. "This is wrong!"

"It's a little late for that argument, don't you think, Princess?"

"I didn't know who you were! I never would have..."

"Never would have rolled in the grass with your stepson?" Faron finished for her.

Tears blurred Belinda's vision. She held herself stiff in Faron's arms. "I don't have to explain anything to you."

"No, you don't," he murmured.

The hardest thing Faron had ever done was to let her go. His body was hard and throbbing with need. It didn't matter one bit that she was his father's widow. But he had to work side by side with her over the next several weeks—or months. It was going to be awkward enough being together every day without knowing for sure that she still desired him as much as he desired her.

"Where do I sleep?" he asked.

Belinda was quivering with relief—or unsatisfied desire. She wasn't willing to examine her feelings closely enough to find out. "Follow me," she said. "I'll show you where your room is."

Once again Faron found himself staring into violet eyes that had turned to ice. He followed her up one half of the curving staircase to a room that might have welcomed some cowboy a hundred years ago. It was furnished sparingly with a maple four-poster, a dry sink, a chest and a rocker. A rag rug covered a small area of the oak hardwood floor. The lamp was electric, but it was Victorian in style.

The connected bathroom had a tub on legs and a pedestal sink. "The linens on the rack are for your use," she said.

Belinda was aware of the confines of the bathroom. She edged her way past the Cowboy and back into the more spacious bedroom. "If you need anything..."

"I'll be fine," Faron said, realizing that she didn't want to spend any more time with him than she had to. "Good night, Princess," he said. His eyes said what he didn't put in words. He wanted her. She was welcome to stay.

Belinda didn't bother to answer. She did what any self-respecting Princess would have done when the dragon started breathing fire. She fled to her room.

Four

Faron was astounded at how much Belinda knew about the business affairs of King's Castle. Unfortunately, the more he learned from her, the more grim-lipped he became. Because things were every bit as bad as she had suggested they were.

"I don't know how you've kept the bank from foreclosing before now," he muttered when he was done examining his father's records.

"Can anything be done to save King's Castle?"

Faron felt his gut tighten as he met Belinda's expectant gaze across the width of the oak rolltop desk in Wayne's study. Even now he wanted her. This morning her golden hair was confined in a single tail that fell over her shoulder, and she was wearing a Western shirt, jeans and boots. She reminded him much too much of his prairie Princess.

He leashed his memories of the previous day and concentrated on the matter at hand. "We can't do it alone," he said. "We'll have to hire some help."

Belinda wiped her palms down the length of her jeans, unaware of the way Faron's gray green eyes followed her gesture. "I don't have money for that."

"I do."

Belinda frowned. "I can't let you spend your money."

"You can't stop me," Faron retorted. "According to my father's will I own half of King's Castle. If something isn't done, the bank is going to take my inheritance. It's no skin off your nose if I invest my money to save my half of this place."

Belinda's lip curled in a wry smile. "You'll also be saving my half," she pointed out.

"I don't want to see my grandmother put out in the street."

Belinda's smile twisted into something more cynical. "And you have to save me to save her, is that it?"

"Something like that."

"Where do we start?" Belinda asked.

Faron arched a disdainful brow. "We?"

"I presume you have some plan in mind. Things that have to be done. I want to help."

"What is it you think you can do?" Faron asked. He preferred to keep her—and temptation—as far from him as possible.

Belinda's chin came up pugnaciously. "What do you need done?"

Faron tried to think of something that would impress upon his stepmother—he had to keep reminding himself how Belinda had deceived him about her identity—how very much *work* was involved in restoring King's Castle to its former greatness.

Not one, but several ideas caught his fancy. He reached out and grabbed Belinda's hand and pulled her after him. "Come with me. I want to start with a tour of the ranch, so I can get some idea of what needs to be done." He only got as far as the back porch before he stopped and asked, "Are there enough roads to get us where we need to go, or should we do this survey on horseback?"

Belinda wasn't sure which was worse. Spending half the day on horseback together would remind them both of the events of the previous day. But if she said they ought to drive, she would have to endure an hour or more confined with him in the cab of a pickup truck. The pickup seemed the lesser of two evils.

"It would be faster and more efficient to drive," she said. "But the only pickup I have isn't in very good mechanical shape."

Faron grimaced at this reminder of the state of poverty in which his father had left his stepmother and grandmother. "We'll take my truck. Just give me a minute to disconnect the horse trailer," he replied.

It was strange seeing King's Castle through Faron's eyes. The splendor of the land, which Belinda had taken for granted, he found not only pleasing to the eye, but a definite economic asset.

"The land itself is a selling point," he explained to her. "It hasn't been overdeveloped. The grass is tall and there's lots of it."

She headed him in the direction of the small herd of Herefords that still roamed King's Castle.

"I see you're using a windmill for water," he said as he pulled the truck to a stop beside the windmill tank.

Faron got out of the truck and headed for the windmill, and Belinda followed after him. He leaned his head back and watched and listened as the wind pushed the windmill around.

"It's not running right," he said at last. "You've got a bolt or two loose up top that ought to be tightened."

She put her hands on her hips. "Who would you suggest I send up there to tighten them. Myself? Or Toby?"

Faron recalled the stature of the stocky cowhand, then gave Belinda a looking over that had a blush skating up her throat. "I guess you," he said at last in a taunting voice.

Belinda's eyes went wide. Was he serious? But if he thought she would back off from such a chore, he had another think coming. "All right," she said, pushing her sleeves up out of the way. "What is it you want me to do?"

Faron pursed his lips in chagrin. He had been certain she would defer the job to him. Now he found himself in the awkward position of having to admit that he had been manipulating the situation. He certainly didn't expect a woman to do the kind of dangerous repair job that was necessary.

He opened his mouth to tell her so and shut it again. The challenging look in her violet eyes dared him to admit he was wrong. Before he conceded the issue, Faron decided to see just how far she was willing to go.

He left Belinda and crossed to the back of his pickup where he kept a tool chest. He rattled around in it for a few moments and came back with a wrench.

"I think this is the tool you'll need."

Belinda took the wrench from him, but she hadn't the slightest idea what to do with it. What she was thinking must have shown in her face, because he stepped up beside her and showed her how to adjust it.

"This way tightens it, this way loosens it. You're not afraid of heights are you?"

Belinda stared at the thin metal ladder that was attached to the windmill. Her eyes followed it what seemed an immense distance into the air. She swallowed and said, "No. I'm not afraid of heights."

"What you're looking for is the bolt that attaches the wheel. Right now the wheel isn't at the correct angle to the yaw axis in the vane."

"What?" Belinda hadn't the vaguest notion what he was talking about.

"You do understand how a windmill works, don't you?"

Belinda wrinkled her nose. "Sort of. I understand the principle of the thing, but not exactly how the pieces fit together."

"Maybe you'd better let me do this." Faron waited for her to concede that he was the one better equipped to handle this job. He had underestimated her stubbornness.

"I can do it," she insisted. "If you'll just explain what it is I have to do."

"That's a little difficult without having the windmill down here where I can point things out," Faron said.

Belinda looked at the ladder. No way could both of them go up it together. "Let me try," she said at last. "If I can't fix it, then you can do the job."

Faron was amazed, but not amused, by Belinda's insistence on climbing to the top of the windmill. "Dammit, woman. It's dangerous to go up there."

"I'm not afraid."

"I am," he muttered. Faron wasn't about to let her endanger her life. "You've proved your point," he said. "You're willing to do what has to be done. Now give me that wrench, and let me go up and tighten that bolt."

"I'm not helpless!"

"I never said you were," Faron retorted. "Now give me the damn wrench!"

Instead, she turned and started up the ladder.

Faron put both arms around her and dragged her back down. Belinda didn't come without a fight. The wrench fell to the ground in the struggle. She kicked and hit at Faron, but he had her from behind and her efforts to free herself were useless.

At last she slumped in his arms.

"Are you done fighting me?" he asked.

"Let me go."

"Are you done fighting me?" he repeated.

"Yessss," she hissed.

Now that he could let her go, Faron realized he didn't want to. His body was way ahead of his mind. It had long since reacted strongly and certainly to the woman in his arms. Faron felt the weight of her soft breasts resting on his forearm. She smelled of soap and shampoo and woman. His hands slid down until his fingertips lay at the base of her belly.

"Faron."

Belinda bit her lip to keep from saying more than Faron's name. Oh, God, she wanted him! She wanted to lie with him, to merge their bodies, to join their souls. But she was not so far gone with desire that she couldn't see the folly of repeating what had happened the previous day.

Belinda covered the male hand on her belly with her own. "We can't do this, Faron. Please. Your father—"

His whole body stiffened. A moment later she was free.

Belinda was afraid to turn around and face him. When she did, she wished she hadn't. There was an awful look of disgust and disdain on his face. The gray green eyes she had found so fascinating yesterday were slicing shards of cut green glass today.

She stooped to pick up the wrench, thus avoiding his piercing gaze. When she rose, she kept her lashes lowered. She held out the wrench, and he took it from her, careful not to touch her hand. Soon after, he was halfway up the ladder.

"Be careful," she whispered. She shaded her eyes from the sun and watched as Faron made his way to the top of the windmill. It didn't take him long to do what he had to do, but Belinda hardly breathed the whole time he was working. He hadn't been kidding about the danger of the job. A fall from that height would break a man in pieces.

When Faron came down the ladder she stayed out of his way. "All finished?"

"That's all I can do right now," he said. "There's a part missing. I'll have to get a replacement."

"Will it cost much?"

"Always thinking about money, Princess?"

"Don't call me that! Not like that!"

"Why not? That's what you are. A pampered, golden Princess. Living off an older man's money—"

"Stop! Stop!" Belinda put her hands to her ears. "How can you be so cruel?"

"Cruel? Princess, I don't hold a candle to you!"

Faron stalked back to the truck. He was furious with himself for losing his temper, for taking out his sexual frustration in such a—yes, cruel—way. He hadn't realized he was capable of that sort of behavior with a woman. Before Belinda . . . Hell, that was a lifetime ago. Before Belinda he had been Faron Whitelaw, happily oblivious to the fact he was Wayne Prescott's son. Before Belinda he had known who he was. Now, everything was so damn confused!

"Get in the truck," he said.

"I'd rather walk back to The Castle than get in that truck with you," Belinda snapped back.

"Listen, Princess. Either you get in that truck under your own steam, or I'm going to pick you up and put you there."

Given that choice, Belinda stomped over to the pickup and got in. He stepped in behind the wheel and gunned the engine. The wheels sent dust flying as they headed down the road.

There was a long silence while both of them fumed. At last Belinda said, "I don't think this is going to work. I think maybe I'll just let the bank take back the ranch. I'll go to work somewhere in town to support myself and Madelyn."

"Doing what?" Faron demanded.

Belinda shrugged. "I used to be a short order cook. I could—"

Faron snorted. "Princesses don't flip hamburgers. Besides, you may be willing to give up your half of this place, but I'm not about to give up my half."

"Now who's thinking about money?" Belinda goaded.

"It's not the money," Faron gritted out. He kept his hands on the wheel and forced himself not to put his foot down on the accelerator. "Oh, hell. I don't have to explain anything to you. Just get the idea of giving this place away out of your head. I'm here and I'm staying until King's Castle is sold. Now, if you're through pouting, maybe you'd like to tell me what else I ought to take a look at."

That was just the beginning of a very long day.

Belinda had put in a lot of hours over the past few years holding King's Castle together, but she had never worked so long or so hard without a rest. She marveled at Faron's energy, at his strength, at his tirelessness. But no matter how many jobs he threw at her, she was determined not to be the one who cried mercy first.

It was nearly dusk when he decided they should clean out the tack room in the barn. The small, windowless room that held saddles, bridles and other leather tack was dark and cool. Belinda pulled a string that lit a single bare bulb hanging overhead. She was assaulted by the pungent smells of leather and horses and, once Faron stepped into the room behind her, hardworking man.

"Some of this leather could use a soaping," Faron said as he walked around the room checking stirrups and reins.

"There hasn't been much time—"

"We'll start now."

"No."

It was the first time since the incident at the windmill that Belinda had objected to anything Faron had suggested. He had been expecting her to quit long before now and head back to the house. She had amazed him with her fortitude. And slowly but surely driven him crazy with her presence.

His body had tightened as he watched her lick off a fine sheen of perspiration on her upper lip that he knew would be salty to the taste. As he watched her stoop and bend and lean in jeans that hugged her rear end like a man's hand. As he watched her cant her head and lift that golden hair up off her neck so the ever-present breeze could cool her, whipping tiny curls across petal-soft skin.

He should be glad she had finally given up, glad she would be out of his hair at long last. Perversely, he said the one thing he believed would provoke her into staying.

"Conceding the battle, Princess?"

Her violet eyes flashed with anger. "I won't dignify that comment with an argument. I'm going to get cleaned up for supper. We can start here tomorrow morning."

When Belinda tried to leave the room, Faron spread his arms and rested his palms on either side of the doorway, blocking the way out.

"Please get out of the way," she said in a controlled voice. "I want to leave."

"You surprised me today."

She arched a brow but said nothing.

"I didn't think you'd be able to keep up all day."

She still said nothing.

"I was wrong."

As an apology it lacked a lot. But it was as much of a concession as Faron was willing to make. "There's something I don't understand," he said.

"What?"

"Why would someone who's willing to work as hard as you have today marry a man twice her age for his money? It doesn't fit."

Belinda's face paled. "It doesn't have to. I don't owe you any explanation. Now let me pass." She wouldn't discuss her marriage to Wayne with Wayne's son. She wouldn't.

When Faron saw she had no intention of answering, he took his weight off his palms and leaned back against the door frame, his legs widespread. She could get out, but not without touching him.

Belinda kept her eyes lowered as she tried to skim past him. She had to turn sideways, and the tips of her breasts brushed his chest. She gasped at her body's reaction to even that brief contact.

Faron's response was powerful and instantaneous. Before Belinda could get past him, he clamped his hands on her shoulders and turned her toward him. His arms folded around her, and he drew her close.

"Faron, don't!"

"Do you think I want to feel like this?" he rasped in her ear. "It's driving me crazy, knowing how your skin tastes, knowing what it feels like to be inside you—and knowing that you were my father's wife!"

Belinda pushed at his chest with the heels of her hands. "Let me go, Faron! This is wrong!"

"You didn't think so yesterday."

"I told you, I didn't know who you were yesterday! This situation is awkward enough. Let's not make it worse."

He nuzzled her temple, let his lips trail down to her ear and felt her shiver in his arms. "And this will make it worse?"

Belinda exhaled a shuddery sigh. "What happened between us was—"

"A miracle."

"A mistake. Faron, we can't let this happen again."

Faron heard the desperation in her voice. He felt the same desperation himself. However, he could afford to be patient. He wasn't going anywhere anytime soon. Neither was she.

He dropped his hands to his sides and stood up straight so there was more space between them. "Call me when supper's ready."

She didn't answer him, just made her escape as quickly as she could. Belinda didn't run back to the house, although it took all her willpower to keep her pace to a walk.

How had things gotten out of hand so quickly? She should have known better than to let herself get cornered like that. But she hadn't been expecting Faron to confront her. She hadn't been expecting him to admit that he still desired her.

But she had been right to push him away. There could be no repetition of what had happened yesterday. Under the circumstances it was unthinkable.

Belinda stepped up on the back porch and shoved her way through the screen door that led to the kitchen. In some ways, the Castle was like any other ranch house. Friends and neighbors always entered through the back door which was usually left open, rather than the front. She stopped dead when she saw Madelyn standing in front of the stove, stirring a pot of chili.

"What are you doing in here?" she asked.

Madelyn lifted a spoonful of chili and sipped a taste of it. "Making supper."

"Where's Rue?"

"She's having one of her spells."

That was Madelyn's way of saying Rue was drunk. Once a year, on the anniversary of her son's death in Vietnam, Rue got drunk. How long the "episode" lasted depended on how good a job Belinda did of finding Rue's stash of bottles and disposing of it. "I thought we'd gotten rid of all the bottles."

"She must have had another tucked away somewhere."

Belinda came up behind Madelyn and put a hand around her shoulder. "You should be resting."

"There'll be time enough for that when I'm laid in my grave."

"I wish you wouldn't talk like that!" Before Wayne's death, Belinda hadn't been quite so aware of Madelyn's mortality. Now she worried about the older woman's health. Madelyn's heart wasn't in much better shape than Wayne's had been.

Madelyn turned and patted Belinda on the arm. "I'm sorry, dear. Why don't you sit down and tell me how the day went with my grandson?"

That brought a wry smile to Belinda's face. "I'll make a deal. *You* sit down, and I'll tell you how the day went."

Madelyn handed over the wooden spoon and took a seat on a bar stool next to the woodblock island in the center of the kitchen. "I'm sitting. Talk."

Belinda turned away to stir the chili, which gave her a chance to organize her thoughts. There was no hope for her feelings, which were still in a state of chaos. "He's a hard worker," Belinda conceded.

"Then you two should have gotten along well," Madelyn said.

Belinda shot Madelyn a look over her shoulder. She was a shrewd old woman. Belinda wondered how much Madelyn knew—or suspected—about the tension between her daughter-in-law and her grandson. "We didn't argue much, if that's what you're getting at." Only at the very beginning and the very end of the day. "Faron has his own way of doing things. I just went along with him."

"Go along and get along. That didn't work very well with Wayne, my dear."

"Faron is nothing like Wayne!" Belinda astonished herself with her outburst. She flushed and tried to backtrack by saying, "I mean, they look nothing alike."

"And they don't act alike, either. Is that what you wanted to say?"

"I don't intend to criticize my late husband to his mother," Belinda said.

Madelyn sighed. "Unfortunately, I'm well aware of my son's faults. I hope you won't let what happened between you and Wayne keep you from finding another young man to love."

Belinda dropped the spoon in the chili and turned to face Madelyn. "I hope you're not thinking about matchmaking, Madelyn. Not matching me with Faron, anyway. For heaven's sake, he's Wayne's son!"

"And quite a good-looking young man, if I do say so myself."

"Please, Madelyn. Don't interfere. Things are difficult enough as it is."

"Difficult? How so?"

Belinda grimaced. She should have known Madelyn wouldn't be satisfied without specifics. But she wasn't going to get them. "We just don't get along."

"It didn't look that way to me last night."

The old woman saw too much. Belinda took a deep breath and let it out. "Suffice it to say that I don't want to get involved with *anyone* right now."

Madelyn was wise enough to know when to let well enough alone. She had said her piece. Not that she wouldn't consider a little manipulating behind the scenes. She would have a talk with her grandson and see which way the wind was blowing.

When the table was set and the corn muffins were just about ready to come out of the oven, Belinda stepped out onto the back porch and circled the triangle hanging from the eave several times with an iron rod. The metallic clang was a sound that cowboys recognized all over the West as a call to supper.

Sure enough, Faron's head and shoulders appeared at the barn door, followed quickly by the rest of him. Belinda knew she should turn around and go back inside, but she couldn't take her eyes off him.

His stride was long and his body moved with an easy grace. His face was hidden by the hat he had pulled down low on his brow. His shirtsleeves were rolled up onto his forearms and she could see the muscles move as he swung his arms in rhythm with his legs. He was almost to the porch by the time she realized he was aware that she had been staring at him.

He stopped with his boot on the first step and tipped his hat back so she could see his face. He was grinning.

"See anything you like?"

"Oh!" She whirled and headed for the door, but she didn't get two steps before he caught her arm and pulled her back around to face him.

"I wasn't complaining. In fact, I'm flattered. I can't keep my eyes off you, either."

"Faron—"

He laid two fingers across her mouth to silence her. His voice was gruff when he spoke again. "You'd better be careful how you look at me with those violet eyes of yours, Princess. I've got myself on a short tether. Don't you go untying any knots."

His fingers slid across her mouth to her cheek, and then tunneled up into her hair. Belinda found herself caught by Faron's green-eyed gaze. It was a powerful force, the desire in a man's eyes. It made a woman want to give herself up to him. Belinda felt her knees growing weak—nature's method of getting a woman down so a man could couple with her more easily. She was having trouble catching her breath, and her mouth dropped open slightly for more air.

Faron saw it differently. He perceived her open mouth as an irresistible invitation. Faron had always liked parties, and he never turned one down. He didn't now.

His head lowered slowly, and his lips parted slightly to match hers. He paused just before their mouths made contact and took a breath. Belinda felt as though he were stealing the breath right out of her. A soft moan sounded deep in her throat.

His lips were pliant against hers. And urgent. She felt his need as his tongue came searching hungrily for sustenance only she could provide. Her hands seemed to have a will of their own. They latched on to his shirt at the waist, then slid up behind his back and threaded into the curls at his nape.

She could feel the dampness where his hair was soaked with sweat. He smelled of hardworking man, a pungent odor, but one that made her think of his muscles bunching beneath cloth as he hefted a bale of hay. His body was hard where he had it pressed against her hips, and his mouth was hot and demanding on hers.

Belinda didn't want to feel so much. Didn't want to need so much. She felt the trap closing on her and at the last minute realized that she must escape. She yanked hard on Faron's hair, and when he howled in pain she let go and backed away as quickly as she could.

"No," she said. "We're not going to do this."

His eyes were feral, his body taut with need. He could still take her if he wanted to. Her aroused, aching body cried out for fulfillment. She saw him hesitate, torn between taking what he wanted or letting her go.

He whirled abruptly and headed for the sink on the back porch. He turned on the cold water full blast, yanked off his hat and threw it down, then stuck his head under the spigot. She stared as he cooled the back of his neck with the icy water. Then he stood and slung his wet hair back. His hands forked through the tangled black curls, setting them in some kind of order. Then he picked up his hat and settled it back on his head.

Water still dripped from his nose and chin and clumped on his eyelashes. But no signs of passion remained when he looked at her again. "You've got some supper ready for me, I believe."

"Yes. I— Yes." She turned and hurried inside, letting the screen door slam behind her. A moment later she heard it creak as he opened it and followed her inside.

Belinda could hardly believe the gentleman who exchanged witticisms with Madelyn at dinner was the same cowboy who had kissed her senseless on the back porch. Faron was absolutely charming. She could see he was good for Madelyn. He made the old woman laugh and even blush once. Asking him to leave was out of the question, even though it was what Belinda desperately wanted to do.

She urged Faron and Madelyn to stay in the dining room and talk while she cleared the table and washed the dishes. But she could hear everything they said through the open door to the kitchen. She cringed when she heard Madelyn ask whether Faron had ever been married.

"No," he answered.

"Why not?" Madelyn asked.

"Never found the right woman, I guess."

"What is it, exactly, you're looking for?"

There was a long pause before he answered, "I'll know her when I find her."

Belinda smiled. Maybe Madelyn had met her match. Faron Whitelaw wasn't the kind of man who could be manipulated. But she should have known her mother-in-law wouldn't easily abandon her matchmaking efforts. Madelyn's next question left Belinda gasping.

"How do you like Belinda?"

"She's a hard worker."

Madelyn chuckled. "She said the same thing about you. I suppose that's one thing you both have in common. I wonder if there are any others."

Again, that long pause.

"I admit I thought Belinda was, well, a little more pampered than she's turned out to be."

"Wayne wasn't the most considerate of husbands."

Belinda gritted her teeth. She wasn't about to let Madelyn start talking about her marriage. She grabbed the apple pie on the counter and marched back through the open doorway. "Dessert, anyone?"

Belinda kept her expression bland, but she had a feeling she wasn't fooling either of them.

"I love apple pie," Faron said. "I'll take a piece. How about you, Maddy?"

Belinda saw the flush rise on Madelyn's cheeks as Faron turned his smile on her.

"Why, I guess I will join you."

Faron turned that stunning smile on Belinda, and she felt—flustered. She dropped the pie on the table and said, "I'll go get some plates and the pie knife.

She turned just in time to keep the two of them from seeing the color race up her throat. This situation was unbearable! She had spent so many years learning to control her emotions, learning to keep what she was feeling hidden, because Wayne inevitably used it against her. All that Cowboy had to do was smile at her and she felt young and foolish again.

And desirable.

Lord, Lord, Lord, he made her feel like he wanted to lick her up like an ice cream cone on a hot Sunday afternoon.

Belinda leaned her forehead against the cool tile wall in the kitchen and took a deep breath. Then she scurried to find plates and a pie server before Faron came looking for her.

She could hear voices again from the other room.

"I'd love to play a little gin rummy," Faron was saying. "Penny a point is fine with me."

"You sure you wouldn't mind?" Madelyn asked.

Belinda could hear the worry in the old woman's voice. Madelyn didn't like being a burden on anyone. She would know if Faron was lying about spending time with her. Belinda heaved a quiet sigh of relief when she heard Faron reply, "Maddy, there's nothing I'd like better than skinning you at gin rummy."

Madelyn giggled. It was a youthful sound and one Belinda couldn't remember ever hearing from the old woman. Had their lives with Wayne been so very grim? It was hard for Belinda to be objective. But hearing Madelyn tonight with her grandson made Belinda wish that things could have been different with Wayne.

She put a smile on her face as she reentered the dining room. "Did I hear you say you're going to challenge Madelyn to a game of rummy?" she asked Faron.

"Yes, ma'am. Soon as I finish my pie."

Belinda served him a piece and set another in front of Madelyn. When she started to leave Faron asked, "Aren't you going to have some, too?"

"I'm not very hungry right now." She kept her lids lowered so Faron wouldn't find out the truth. She wanted to get away now, while she could still think rationally. She didn't want to see him being nice to his grandmother. She didn't want to see him being charming. She wanted to remember who he was and who she was and why any relationship between them other than the legal one resulting from her marriage to Faron's father was a mistake.

"I'm a little tired. I thought I'd go to bed early tonight," she said.

She was unprepared when Faron left the table and crossed to her. He stood facing her and said in a voice too low to carry back to Madelyn, "Are you all right?"

She felt breathless again. "Yes. I'm fine. Just a little tired."

He put a hand on her shoulder, and she felt the pressure of it deep in the pit of her belly.

"I made some calls while you were having lunch and hired some men to do the heavy labor. There's no reason for you to leave the house tomorrow."

Her eyes flashed up to meet his concerned gaze. "I'll do my part," she said.

"You don't—"

"I don't want any favors from you. I'll see you tomorrow morning."

Belinda jerked herself away and marched toward the spiral staircase. She felt Faron's eyes on her the entire way up to the second floor. When she reached her room, she closed the door behind her and leaned against it.

She felt like crying. Why hadn't she met Faron Whitelaw eight years ago? It was too late now for what might have been. And what made her think things would be any different with Faron? She had learned her lessons from Wayne. Things had been fine with him, too, at first. It was only later...

But Wayne Prescott had never made her feel the things Faron Whitelaw made her feel. Belinda was frightened. And excited. She felt a sort of anticipation for the days to come that she knew was dangerous for her peace of mind. Worst of all was the knowledge that she desired Faron Whitelaw every bit as much as he seemed to desire her.

She had to resist temptation. She had to make herself a regal, unapproachable Princess. Maybe that would keep the Cowboy at bay.

Belinda lifted her chin and focused her eyes on the distant canopy bed with its delicate eyelet covers. It was a bed eminently fit for a princess who had resigned herself to life in an inaccessible, remote ivory tower.

She crossed the room and sat down on the bed with her back stiff and her teeth clenched to still a quivering chin. She had survived a lot over the past eight years. By God, she would survive this as well.

Five

Over the next several weeks, Belinda kept her distance from Faron. She conversed with him at breakfast, where Madelyn provided a buffer, and he gave her jobs so she could contribute to the work being accomplished at King's Castle. But nothing she did brought her into contact with Faron.

She marveled at the improvements in the ranch. Fences lost their dilapidated look, buildings got a new coat of paint, windmills began to whir again, machinery had a well-oiled sound. She began to believe that they really might find a buyer for the ranch. And to realize that if—when—King's Castle was finally sold, she was going to miss it.

One of her jobs today was to oil all the hinges on the stalls. Belinda thought she was alone in the barn, so she practically jumped out of her skin when a voice behind her said, "What are you doing?"

She whirled, then expelled a relieved breath. "You scared me half to death!"

Faron grinned. "I usually have a somewhat different effect on women. So what are you doing?" he asked again.

She held out the oil can so he could see it. "I'm doing just what you ordered me to do this morning."

"Ordered?"

"All right, what you *suggested* I do."

He took the can out of her hand and set it on the corner of one of the stalls. "Madelyn sent me to get you. She said she needs you in the house."

If Belinda thought that keeping distance between them had diffused the sexual tension one whit, she was finding out now that she had been wrong. She was aware of Faron from the top of her head to the tips of her toes. "Did she say why she wants me?"

"No. But I noticed there's a lot of cleaning going on in the house. I asked Rue what was going on, and she said we're expecting company."

"My sisters and their families always come to King's Castle to visit during the Fourth of July holiday."

"Now I remember. You said something about that the first day—" He cut himself off. He didn't want to think back to the day he had met Belinda, when they had shared a special moment in time together. He had been trying desperately over the past couple of weeks to treat her like the stepmother she was.

It wasn't working. All he had to do was take a breath around her, and his body surged to life. He had given her things to do that would keep them apart, but once her family arrived they would be forced into social situations together. It would be hell pretending in front of her family that he didn't want her.

"When does your family start arriving?"

"Tomorrow."

Faron took off his hat, forked his fingers through his hair and tugged the hat back on again. "You could have given me a little more warning."

"Why? There's nothing you need to do. Madelyn and Rue and I will take care of everything."

If he'd had more warning maybe he could have figured out a reason to be gone from the ranch during their visit. If he left now it would look like he was running. Faron wasn't the kind of man to run from trouble. Not that he necessarily sought it out, either. But he could see trouble coming.

Still, some good might come of this visit. He would have a chance to ask Belinda's family some of the questions she had refused to answer. "I'm looking forward to meeting your sisters.''

Belinda smiled. ''It'll be hard not to trip over them, since they'll all be staying at the house.''

By sundown the next day Faron realized that Belinda hadn't been exaggerating. Her three sisters, Dori, Tillie and Fiona, had all arrived. Dori had come with her husband, Bill, and three daughters under seven years of age. Tillie was also married. She and her husband, Sam, had two boys, five and nine. Fiona was still single, but she had brought her Abyssinian cat, Tutankhamen, Tut for short.

There were trucks on the floor, dolls on the chairs and screaming children chasing each other and the cat up and down the stairs. When they all sat down to dinner it was chaos.

It reminded Faron of home. Of the days when his mother had still been alive, and he and his brothers had argued at the table while their parents refereed. He felt his stomach twist when he realized that the picture he remembered hadn't been exactly as it had seemed.

Had his father's eyes been sad as they met his mother's across the table? Had there been any hesitancy in the way his father had lifted him up into his arms and held him in his lap? He couldn't remember.

Whatever his father had felt about raising another man's child hadn't been evident in the way Faron had been treated. He had felt loved, had known he was loved. By a woman who had been faithless to his father in conceiving him. By a man who had overlooked the foreign blood that ran in his veins.

He sat back and listened to the children around him and searched for the warm memories he knew he would find.

"Mom, Travis threw a pea at me!"

"Travis, stop throwing food at Peter."

"Dad, make Jennifer stop kicking the table."

"Jennifer, that's enough. Eat."

"Daddy, Trisha spilled her milk."

"I did not!"

"It's all over your dress."

"Is not!"

"Is, too!"

"Is not!"

"Penny! Trisha! That's enough from both of you. Can't we have a little peace and quiet here?"

No, Faron thought. There would be no peace and quiet until the kids had been put to bed. But he didn't mind. And he could see that Belinda didn't mind, either. In fact, the look in her eyes was decidedly soft—and yearning.

He remembered what Belinda had said about wanting children. He wondered why she and his father hadn't given him stepbrothers and stepsisters. Suddenly he was fiercely, selfishly glad that Belinda hadn't borne his father's children. Even if it meant she had no child to hold to her breast during this family reunion. Because he wanted to be the one to give her those children.

Until that moment Faron hadn't realized how deep his feelings for Belinda ran. He had known, of course, that he desired her physically. When he looked at her now it was with the knowledge that she was the one woman he was meant to spend his life with. With a sense of awful frustration he conceded that the unique relationship that had brought them together was equally likely to be what kept them apart.

Faron turned his gaze on Belinda. She had settled Jennifer, the youngest of Dori's daughters, in her lap and was playing patty-cake with the child. The smile on Belinda's face was easily as broad as the little girl's. When Jennifer threw her hands wide, Belinda tossed her head back to keep from getting hit. And met Faron's eyes.

He made no effort to hide what he was feeling. At first her expression softened. She shared with him the joy of holding the baby in her arms. As he continued staring, she lowered her lids and hid those expressive violet eyes from him. But it was too late. He had already seen the need, the desire, the yearning for a child of her own.

"Time for baths," Tillie announced.

"Aw, Mom!"

"Jeez, Mom!"

"I want to play some more."

Faron listened to all the complaints knowing that they were being made in vain. The children's parents slowly but surely herded their offspring up the stairs. He wasn't surprised when Belinda took advantage of the opportunity to escape with them. Madelyn excused herself to check on Rue, who had apparently found another bottle this afternoon.

That left Faron sitting at the table with Belinda's youngest sister, Fiona. Fiona had a pixie face, and from what Faron had seen, a puckish sense of humor. She was blond and blue-eyed, but considerably shorter than her eldest sister. She had a figure that curved in all the right places. If Faron had met her before Belinda, he might even have been interested in getting to know her better.

Fiona picked up her wineglass and walked down the length of the table to take a chair across from Faron. "I guess you and I are the only ones without someone to bathe." She paused and added with a come-hither smile, "Unless you'd like me to scrub your back?"

"No thanks," Faron said, returning the smile.

"Thank goodness."

"Pardon?"

Fiona's smile turned into a grin. "I was just checking. I mean, I saw the way you stared at Belinda all night. You wouldn't be the right kind of guy for her if you were willing to hustle me the minute her back was turned."

"Thanks for the vote of confidence."

"Oh, I'm still not sure you're what she needs."

"And what is that?"

Fiona's blue eyes bored into him. Her hands fisted on the table. "Someone who wouldn't take advantage of her. Someone who would make her happy."

"She wasn't happy with my father?"

Fiona gave an unladylike snort. "Not hardly."

Faron waited for her to say more. He didn't have to wait long.

"Wayne Prescott abused my sister. Oh, not so much physically. Although I know he hit her once or twice. But he crushed her spirit. Or at least he tried. Toward the end Belinda learned to hide what she was feeling, and he left her alone."

Faron felt a rage such as he had never known directed at a man who was beyond his reach. "Why didn't she leave him?"

"I asked her the same question. She said they had made a deal, and she owed him her loyalty."

"What kind of deal?"

Fiona's eyes were bleak. "Belinda sold herself to get the money to take care of us. Me and Dori and Tillie. When she married Wayne he established a substantial trust fund in each of our names. Dori went to UCLA and fell in love with Bill. Tillie married the doctor who put the cast on the broken leg she got skiing in Colorado. I bought a bed and breakfast in Vermont. Belinda got nothing. Except marriage to Wayne.

"Of course, all of us were too young to realize what she was doing when she did it. She told us she was in love with Wayne, and during the first couple of years they got along pretty well."

"What happened then?"

"Wayne started to gamble. He lost big. He took it out on Belinda. He kept her like a prisoner here, wouldn't let her go anywhere. I guess he was afraid she wouldn't come back. If it hadn't been for Madelyn, she probably would have left him."

"What does Madelyn have to do with anything?"

"You've seen them together. Madelyn treats Belinda like the daughter she never had, and Belinda returns her affection. They both tried to curb Wayne's excesses. Sometimes I think if Belinda hadn't been there, Wayne might have taken out his frustrations on his mother."

"Not the best father figure a man could have."

"I'm sorry. I forgot he was your father. But he wasn't really, was he? I mean, someone else raised you. You're certainly nothing like Wayne from what I've seen today."

"The question is whether Belinda sees my father when she looks at me," Faron said.

"I don't see how she could," Fiona said. "You don't look a thing like him. You don't act like him, either. Wayne mostly thought about himself. From things Belinda has told me about you—"

"Belinda talked to you about me?"

Fiona shrugged. "She just told me you were Wayne's son." Belinda had revealed a whole lot more about her feelings for Faron Whitelaw through what she had not said. But Fiona wasn't about to give away Belinda's secrets to the cowboy. She would keep her eyes open over the next couple of days and make her own judgment about whether Faron deserved a chance with Belinda.

"Guess I'd better go see if I can help get things settled upstairs. I'll be down later to help with the dishes," Fiona said.

Faron looked around him and realized everything was still sitting on the table. With Rue sleeping off her latest binge there was no one to handle such details. "I'll take care of it," Faron said.

Thus, when Belinda came downstairs she found the table cleared, the leftovers put away and Faron wiping down the counters with a sponge.

"You didn't have to do the dishes," she protested. "I would have done them."

"You were busy. I didn't mind. Charlie One-Horse taught me how to stack a dishwasher."

"Who's Charlie One-Horse?"

"A cross between hired hand, mother and father at Hawk's Way. He kind of takes care of things."

Belinda sat on one of the bar stools at the center island and leaned her chin on the heel of her hand. "When you see Charlie again, tell him I said thanks. I have to admit I'm a little tired."

"You work too hard."

"It was mostly play today. I love having my family around, but they keep things hectic."

"I spent some time after dinner talking to Fiona."

Belinda's lids lowered to hide her eyes. "And?"

"She told me why you married my father."

"Fiona never could keep a secret."

"She's grateful for what you did."

Belinda's voice was bitter as she explained. "If I had it to do over again, I wouldn't. And I won't make the same mistake twice. I'll never let another man do to me what Wayne did. I won't—"

Belinda suddenly realized who she was talking to. Wayne's son. A man it would be all too easy to allow into her life. Would she be making a mistake if she did? Or would things be different with Faron? She wished . . . she wished . . .

"Excuse me." Abruptly Belinda stood and headed for the screen door. She shoved her way outside and started walking. She didn't have any destination in mind, she just wanted to get away. Belinda didn't want to think of might-have-beens. She was tired of feeling regret. It wouldn't change what had happened. She had to forget about the past and go on with her life. Alone. That was the safest way, the best way to survive.

Faron stood in the kitchen after Belinda was gone, thinking back over what he had learned about her marriage to his father.

Belinda might have married Wayne Prescott for money, but she had done it from self*less* rather than self*ish* motives. It had become increasingly clear to him that she had bought security for her sisters at a very high price.

Now that he knew Belinda bitterly regretted what she had done, he allowed himself to acknowledge that he had been jealous of her relationship with his father. He wanted Belinda's love unbound by memories of her past. He was grateful to learn that he didn't have to compete with loving recollections of Wayne Prescott. But it had dawned on him this evening that he might have even more difficulty overcoming the damage done by his father's abusive treatment of his wife.

I won't make the same mistake twice. I'll never let another man do to me what Wayne did.

Faron was going to have to prove to Belinda that he wasn't like his father. That he was capable of loving her, of cherishing her, of treating her with the respect she deserved. He had to find a way to convince her that marriage to him wouldn't even remotely resemble her relationship with his father.

There was no time like the present to start.

Faron shoved open the screen door and marched out into the darkness after Belinda. She had already disappeared beyond the light pouring from the windows. He increased his pace and finally caught up to her at the edge of the river that ran across King's Castle.

The North Platte was narrow here, and the shallow water rushed over stones that made up the riverbed. Cottonwoods lined the water, and their leaves rustled in the wind. A zephyr cooled the night air. The cicadas chirped, and Faron heard an owl hoot in the distance. They might have been two people lost on the prairie with no one around for a thousand miles.

Or so it felt.

The moonlight created a glow around Belinda, outlining her so she was easy to find. "Why did you run away?"

Belinda whirled, surprised to find she had been followed. "I thought it was pretty obvious why I left. I was telling my late husband's son that his father was a terrible husband. Not the most proper after-dinner conversation I can imagine."

"But fascinating all the same."

"Why don't you go away and leave me alone? I've made up my mind not to get involved with another man—ever."

Her statement seemed to confirm his fears and left him feeling angry over what he couldn't control. "Are you only precluding marriage? Or do you plan to live the rest of your life as celibate as a nun?"

Belinda crossed her arms defensively. "I don't think that's any of your business."

"There you're wrong. Because," he said in a low, dangerous voice, "you're lying to yourself if you think you can live without love for the rest of your life."

"I don't need a man—for any reason."

"I think you're lying. To me. And to yourself." Faron stalked her now as he had wanted to for the past month. He was fighting for their life together. This time he wouldn't allow her to escape.

Belinda backed away slowly, but for every step she took, Faron took two. She found herself backed up against a cottonwood at the edge of the river with nowhere else to retreat.

Faron laid his palms on the bark on either side of her head and leaned down so they were eye to eye. "I'm not my father. I would never hurt you."

"That's what you say now," Belinda said in a tremulous voice. "But later—"

"Later I'll be the same man I am now. A man who desires you, Princess. A man who wants to cherish you."

It was too much what she had always wanted to hear from a man she cared for, and never had. Belinda's eyes sank closed. A moment later she felt Faron's mouth on hers. Gentle. Tender. Coaxing.

He insinuated his body between her thighs and rubbed himself against her. "Princess, open your mouth for me. Please."

He caught her upper lip with his teeth and teased it, then slid his tongue along the crease of her lips, making her gasp with the pleasure of it. He took advantage of the opportunity to slip his tongue inside, to taste, to tempt her to join him in his sensual exploration.

She put her palms on his chest, intending to push him away, but her fingers curled against the cloth instead, and she pulled him closer. Faron's arms curved around her and aligned them from breast to hip.

"I need you, Princess."

Belinda caught fire in Faron's arms. There was no denying that she wanted him. And needed him. As the prairie grass needed sunshine. As the flowers needed spring rain. Her knees would no longer support her, and she and Faron sank to the ground together.

Faron made short work of Belinda's blouse, but when he reached under her skirt he found a delightful surprise. "You're wearing nylons."

"I always wear nylons with a skirt."

Faron grinned. "I mean real nylons." His hand slid around the top rim of her nylons and followed the garter belt up to her waist. "It's been a long time since I've met a woman who wore a garter belt."

"So I'm old-fashioned. Sue me."

"I'd rather make love to you."

Faron took his time removing her nylons. By the time he had her garter belt off, they were both having trouble breathing. He unsnapped his shirt and then pulled it off over his head. He unbuckled his belt, but when he reached for the zipper, she was there before him.

She took her time, touching him as she had always dreamed of touching a man. Aware of his guttural groans of pleasure, aware of the restraint he exercised to remain quiescent under her touch. But soon, touching wasn't enough for either of them. Faron finished what Belinda had started, and in moments they were both naked in the moonlight.

"You're so beautiful," Faron said. "So exquisite."

Belinda had never felt so loved, so cared for, so much the object of a man's desire. She ran her hands across his broad shoulders, feeling the play of muscle and sinew. Then her hands slipped up his back and tunneled into his hair. She urged his head down until their mouths met.

It was a kiss of longing. Of belonging. Her to him. Him to her. It was more than sex. It always had been. It always would be. Something magical, something mystical happened between them when their bodies merged. Their souls meshed, as well.

When at last they lay sated in each other's arms, Belinda didn't feel grateful to Faron for proving her wrong about needing him. She hated him for being right. Because she was afraid to take another chance. The consequences of her relationship with Faron's father were too devastating ever to forget.

She sat up with her back to Faron and began putting her clothes on. "This doesn't change anything."

Faron sat up, but made no move to touch her. "What do you mean?"

"I'm not going to let myself get involved with you."

"You already are involved!" Faron retorted. "You can't pretend nothing just happened between us."

"It was just sex."

"Like hell it was!" Faron was angry. Even though he knew why Belinda was shoving him away, it didn't make the rejection any less painful. He stood and slipped on his shorts, then yanked on his jeans. "I know you had a tough time with my father, but I thought we'd settled all that."

"I can't take the chance you'll turn out to be like him," Belinda said in a quiet voice.

"I'm not—"

"You're an especially bad risk, Faron. After all, like father, like son."

Belinda could see Faron was furious. She waited for a blow that never came. Instead, he sat back down, pulled on his socks and boots, then stood and retrieved his shirt without saying another word.

He wasn't like his father. She knew it. And he knew it. Yet he didn't argue with her. When he was finished dressing he turned to her and said, "I'll walk you back to the house."

"I don't need—"

"Don't argue with me, Princess."

She didn't. She stuffed her nylons and garter belt into the pocket of her denim skirt, stuck her bare feet into her shoes and headed back toward the house.

The house was dark when they returned. Apparently both adults and children had welcomed the day's end. Belinda began to think she might escape to her bedroom without any further confrontation with Faron. She almost did.

At the top of the stairs Faron caught her hand and drew her toward him.

"It was beautiful, Princess. What happened between us was beautiful. I don't know what my father did to you. I don't even want to try to imagine what it must have been like living with him. But I don't intend to let what happened between the two of you interfere with our relationship."

"But—"

He put his fingertips to her lips. "All men aren't like my father. Not even his son. Especially not his son."

He let her go, and she disappeared into her bedroom. A moment later Faron found himself facing Belinda's sister, Fiona. Faron held his breath, waiting for whatever she had to say.

"I didn't mean to eavesdrop. I was looking for Tut." The Abyssinian curled himself around her

NO COST! NO OBLIGATION TO BUY!
NO PURCHASE NECESSARY!

PLAY "LUCKY 7"
AND GET AS MANY AS FIVE FREE GIFTS . . .

HOW TO PLAY:

1. With a coin, carefully scratch off the silver box at the right. This makes you eligible to receive two or more free books, and possibly another gift, depending on what is revealed beneath the scratch-off area.

2. Send back this card and you'll receive brand-new Silhouette Desire® novels. These books have a cover price of $2.89 each, but they are yours to keep absolutely free.

3. There's no catch. You're under no obligation to buy anything. We charge nothing—ZERO—for your first shipment. And you don't have to make any minimum number of purchases—not even one!

4. The fact is thousands of readers enjoy receiving books by mail from the Silhouette Reader Service™ months before they're available in stores. They like the convenience of home delivery and they love our discount prices!

5. We hope that after receiving your free books you'll want to remain a subscriber. But the choice is yours—to continue or cancel, anytime at all! So why not take us up on our invitation, with no risk of any kind. You'll be glad you did!

You'll look like a million dollars when you wear this lovely necklace! Its cobra-link chain is a generous 18" long, and the multi-faceted Austrian crystal sparkles like a diamond!

DETACH AND MAIL CARD TODAY

PLAY "LUCKY 7"

**Just scratch off the silver box with a coin.
Then check below to see which gifts you get.**

YES! I have scratched off the silver box. Please send me all the gifts for which I qualify. I understand I am under no obligation to purchase any books, as explained on the back and on the opposite page.

225 CIS AJDP
(U-SIL-D-05/93)

NAME

ADDRESS   APT

CITY   STATE   ZIP

7 7 7	**WORTH FOUR FREE BOOKS PLUS A FREE CRYSTAL PENDANT NECKLACE**	
🍒 🍒 🍒	**WORTH THREE FREE BOOKS PLUS A FREE CRYSTAL PENDANT NECKLACE**	
● ● ●	**WORTH THREE FREE BOOKS**	
🔔 🔔 🍒	**WORTH TWO FREE BOOKS**	

THE SILHOUETTE READER SERVICE™: HERE'S HOW IT WORKS

Accepting free books puts you under no obligation to buy anything. You may keep the books and gift and return the shipping statement marked "cancel." If you do not cancel, about a month later we will send you 6 additional novels, and bill you just $2.24 each plus 25¢ delivery and applicable sales tax, if any.* That's the complete price, and—compared to cover prices of $2.89 each—quite a bargain! You may cancel at any time, but if you choose to continue, every month we'll send you 6 more books, which you may either purchase at the discount price . . . or return at our expense and cancel your subscription.

* Terms and prices subject to change without notice. Sales tax applicable in N.Y.

BUSINESS REPLY MAIL
FIRST CLASS MAIL   PERMIT NO. 717   BUFFALO NY

POSTAGE WILL BE PAID BY ADDRESSEE

SILHOUETTE READER SERVICE
3010 WALDEN AVE
PO BOX 1867
BUFFALO NY 14240-9952

NO POSTAGE
NECESSARY
IF MAILED
IN THE
UNITED STATES

bare ankles and purred. "I think maybe you'll do for Belinda. I think maybe you'll do just fine."

Faron smiled grimly. "All I have to do now is convince your sister of that."

"You'll manage. Be patient. All it'll take is a little time." She leaned down and picked up the cat, then closed the door, shutting Faron out.

Faron stared down the hall at Belinda's closed door. He didn't have as much time as Fiona seemed to think. With the progress he was making turning the ranch into a showplace, they were bound to find a buyer soon. Once they sold the ranch, he would head back to Texas.

If he didn't get matters resolved with Belinda, he was likely to end up making the trip alone.

Faron clenched his fists in determination.

He would be damned if he'd leave her behind.

Six

Belinda managed to avoid Faron until her sisters left. She knew he was giving her space. Fiona had told her so—and a lot more besides—while they were sitting at the Casper airport. Dori's and Tillie's flights had already come and gone. She was waiting for Fiona's plane to depart.

"You can't judge every man by your husband," Fiona had said.

"What other gauge would you suggest I use?" Belinda demanded.

"Your heart."

"I don't have one."

Fiona laughed. "Don't you wish! You've got one all right. Maybe a little bruised and battered, but it's in there beating away. And if what I suspect is true, beating a whole lot faster whenever a certain cowboy is around."

Belinda was helpless to control the flush that rose on her cheeks. "All right, so I'm attracted to Faron Whitelaw. He's a handsome man."

"And charming."

"And charming. But he's also my stepson."

"A fact that makes absolutely no difference."

"How can you say that?"

"It might be different if Faron had grown up at King's Castle, if you had stood in the role of stepmother and he had been your stepson. But that wasn't the case.

"You know what I think, Belinda? I think the fact Faron is technically your stepson is just an excuse."

Belinda laughed nervously. "An excuse for what?"

"An excuse not to fall in love with him. Which you already half are, if I'm not mistaken."

That nervous laugh escaped again. Belinda lowered her eyelids to hide her expressive eyes, but Fiona exercised the prerogative of younger sisters the world over to ignore her elder sister's tender sensibilities.

"Look," Fiona said. "I say you ought to go for it."

Belinda gasped. "*Go for it?* What kind of thing is that to urge your sister to do?"

"Look, you like the guy, right?"

Fiona didn't wait for Belinda to respond.

"And he likes you."

Again Fiona didn't wait for Belinda to respond.

"So go for it. Give the relationship a chance. Get to know Faron. Let yourself fall in love—I mean, if that's what happens."

"And if nothing happens?"

"Then you're no worse off than you were before," Fiona said philosophically.

Fiona's flight was called. She rose and hugged Belinda, then picked up the cat carrier that held Tut. "Be happy, Belinda. You deserve it. Call me, okay?"

"Okay."

Belinda waved as Fiona turned and smiled over her shoulder. Before Fiona even got to the door, she had met a man traveling on the same flight. Belinda shook her head in disbelief at her sister's easy way with men as she turned and headed for the parking lot. But she used the drive back from Casper to think about Fiona's advice.

Be happy, Belinda. You deserve it.

It was wonderful advice, actually. If only Belinda knew what would make her happy, she would do it. The problem was, Belinda had no idea what she wanted. She had been honest with Faron the day she had met him. She hadn't ever allowed herself to dream. Right after her parents were buried, she had needed to work to support her sisters. After she had married Wayne, whatever hopes she'd harbored had died a sure, if not precisely sudden, death.

So what would make her happy?

A husband who loved her. A houseful of children, with Madelyn nearby, a doting grandmother.

It was all so very simple. The Princess would just fall in love with the Cowboy and live happily ever after.

But as Belinda drove up to The Castle, the old fears rose up before her. How could she be sure things would turn out happily ever after? Was she willing to take the risk of loving Faron? They had been forced by circumstance into each other's company. What if the ranch sold in the next few weeks? Would he leave her behind and return to Texas without another thought of her?

Belinda found Faron sitting in one of the rockers on the stone terrace along the side of the house with Madelyn sitting in the rocker beside him. The sun was just setting, and in the fading light Belinda saw that Madelyn's head was thrown back and she was laughing. Belinda wanted to be a part of that picture.

When she stopped the pickup, Faron bounded down from the terrace, pulled open the door and practically dragged her out.

"Come on and join us," he said. "We're having a glass of tea and exchanging war stories."

"War stories?" Belinda felt the strength in Faron's hand as he gripped her fingers and tugged her along behind him.

And yet she knew how gentle he could be. Surely he wasn't like his father. Surely...

Faron seated her in the rocker where he had been sitting and settled himself on the flagstone terrace cross-legged facing her. "I just finished my war story," he said. "It's Maddy's turn."

"What kind of war story?" Belinda persisted.

"Be still and listen, girl, and you'll find out soon enough," Madelyn chided with a twinkle in her eye. "Now, let's see. It must have been '42, or maybe it was '43. Everyone contributed what he or she could to the War Effort. I did my part. I danced for the USO."

"I didn't know there was a USO in Casper," Belinda said.

"Hush, girl," Madelyn said. "This is my story." She leaned back in the rocker and set it in motion with the toe of her shoe.

"His name was Tommy Neville. He had the bluest eyes and the blackest hair I'd ever seen. We met at the USO. He was a Navy flier headed to California, scheduled to ship out to the Pacific. It was his last night at home. He said he wanted to hold an American girl in his arms one last time, and feel the touch of her lips on his—because he might not be coming home.''

''What a line!'' Faron interjected. ''So did you kiss him?''

''What kind of war stories *are* these?'' Belinda asked suspiciously.

''Hush, dear, and let me finish,'' Maddy reproved. ''Of course I kissed him,'' she said with a girlish grin. ''What kind of patriot would I have been if I'd let a soldier go off to war without a goodbye kiss?''

Faron clapped his hands. ''Good for you, Maddy. Your turn, Belinda.''

''My turn for what?''

''We're telling romantic war stories,'' Maddy explained. ''Your turn.''

''I . . . I wasn't dating anyone during a war.''

Faron and Maddy exchanged disbelieving looks and then burst out laughing.

''She can't be that naive, can she?'' Faron asked Maddy.

''I wouldn't have said so, but maybe she is. Perhaps you'd better explain it to her.''

''We're telling 'war' stories about our previous love affairs,'' Faron said.

''You're exchanging romantic escapades with your *grandmother?*'' Belinda asked incredulously. ''Whose idea was this?''

''Mine,'' Madelyn said.

That took the wind out of Belinda's sails.

"So, are you going to play or not?" Madelyn asked.

"I'm not!"

"Chicken!" Faron taunted.

"Coward!" Madelyn accused.

"All right!" Belinda retorted. "You asked for it. You're going to get it!"

"I can't wait to hear this," Faron said, settling back against the short stone wall that edged the terrace.

"Me, either," Madelyn said with a chuckle.

"He had the biggest, brownest eyes you ever saw."

"You like brown eyes?" Faron asked with a frown.

"Shut up and listen," Belinda said. "And he had curly red hair."

"So tell us about the date," Faron urged.

"We spent the whole night together," Belinda said.

Faron's eyes narrowed. "The whole night? Who the hell was this guy?"

"His name was Whitey."

"What kind of name is that for a redheaded man?" Faron asked disgustedly.

"It's a terrible name for a man," Belinda agreed. "But a great name for a Hereford steer."

"A steer?"

Belinda saw the moment when recognition—and relief—dawned on Faron's face.

Madelyn joined Faron's laughter. "I guess she showed us."

Belinda was glad they believed she had told her story as a joke. Because the truth was, there weren't any other men in her life. Not that she was embarrassed to admit to her lack of experience. No wonder she was afraid to take a chance on romantic love. Having never felt the emotion, she wasn't sure she would recognize it if it bit her on the nose.

"I'm going in to see if Rue needs any help," Madelyn said.

Faron jumped up to help his grandmother out of the rocker.

"You'd think I was an old lady," she muttered.

"No, just a lady," Faron said with a gentle smile.

Madelyn shot a look at Belinda as though to say, "You're a fool if you don't grab him!"

When Madelyn was gone, Faron took her seat and set the rocker in motion. Belinda joined him rocking, and the only sound for a while was the creak of the wooden rockers and the occasional lowing of cattle.

"Did you have a nice drive back from Casper?"

"Yes."

"I like your sisters."

"They are nice, aren't they?"

"Was the sacrifice worth it?"

Belinda sighed. "It was a foolish thing to do. Everything turned out better than I had a right to expect."

"Meaning your sisters ended up happy, even if you didn't."

Belinda didn't bother to respond because Faron hadn't been asking a question, he had been making a statement. The two of them rocked quietly, each caught up in his own thoughts.

Faron's sister Tate had called while Belinda was at the airport. It had been one of the most difficult conversations of Faron's life.

"I called Hawk's Way looking for you," Tate began, "because Adam and I want you to be our son's godfather. Garth said you'd gone to Wyoming, but he wouldn't tell me why. He just gave me this number and said you'd answer my questions. So what are you doing in Wyoming, Faron?"

Faron felt a lump in his throat. This is what it meant to be a part of the Whitelaw family. Caring. Concern. Curiosity. But he didn't have the right to play the role she wanted to cast him in without confessing the truth first. "Tate, I—"

She was too impatient to allow him to get a word in edgewise. "Spill the beans, big brother. What's going on up there? I'm guessing there's a woman involved. Am I right?"

Tate had been talking virtually without taking a breath, so when she finally stopped, the silence was awesome.

"Faron? Is something wrong? Talk to me."

Faron realized Garth had left it up to him to decide whether to tell the rest of the family the truth about his birth. For a moment he thought about making up some kind of story to hide what their mother had done. But Tate was a mother herself now. She was no longer a child who had to be protected from the facts of life.

"I'm here in Wyoming to meet my stepmother."

There was an absurdly long silence on the other end of the line.

"Is this some kind of joke, Faron? I don't understand."

Faron heard Tate's confusion, her anger and her fear. He shoved his free hand through his hair. "It's no joke, Tate. Mother had an affair before you were born. I was the result. My real father left me half his ranch in Wyoming. I came up here to...to see this place."

"Am I...?"

"You're legitimate, as far as I know," Faron reassured her. "I guess Mom and Dad got back together after her affair."

"I'm so sorry, Faron."

Faron swallowed over the lump in his throat. "I'll understand if you don't want me to be godfather to—"

"Oh, no! Please, Faron. You *have* to be the baby's godfather. It's what Adam and I both want. This other...thing...doesn't change how I feel about you. You're still my brother, and I love you dearly."

Faron's eyes burned with tears. He wanted to tell Tate how much her love meant to him but he couldn't get the words past his constricted throat.

"Faron? Are you there?"

At last he managed, "I'm here, Tate."

"Well, will you do it? Will you be Brett's godfather?"

"I'd be proud and pleased to be godfather to your son."

He heard a sigh of relief on the other end of the line.

"Everybody's coming to Hawk's Way over Labor Day. That's not a problem for you, is it? Because if it is, we can change the day. We need you there."

"I can make it. I might bring a couple of people along."

"So there *is* a girl involved!"

Faron grinned. "Maybe."

"I can't wait to meet her. What's she like?"

"Goodbye, Tate."

"Goodbye, Faron. And thanks again. I love you. See you at Hawk's Way. Oh. Wait. Does Jesse know?"

"I haven't said anything to him."

"Do you want me to tell him?"

Faron thought how easy it would be to say yes. "No. I'll call him. Goodbye, Tate."

"Goodbye."

Faron hadn't waited to make the call to Jesse. It seemed better to get it over with right away. Jesse was considerably more philosophical than Faron had expected him to be.

"I'm not surprised," Jesse had said.

"You're not?"

"I'm older than you. I guess I saw more than you did as a child. Mom and Dad...there were some arguments, some hard words. It went on for about a year. Then it suddenly stopped. That must have been when she was having the affair. Their marriage seemed stronger after that."

Faron marveled at how differently his two older brothers had viewed their mother's infidelity. Garth remembered only the hurt. Jesse had remembered the healing. Surprisingly, Faron felt better knowing that his illegitimate birth hadn't split his parents apart, but might even have helped draw them closer together.

Faron had hung up the phone feeling like a huge weight had been lifted from his shoulders, one he hadn't even been aware he was carrying around.

Remembering the two phone calls reminded Faron that he had already set in motion plans to get Belinda to visit Hawk's Way. Now all he had to do was convince her she should go.

"I think you'd like my brothers and sister if you ever met them," Faron said, breaking the peaceful silence between them.

Belinda was still half dreaming and murmured, "Maybe I will someday."

"How about Labor Day?"

Belinda put out a foot to stop her rocker. "What?"

"I got a call while you were gone to the airport. The family is getting together for the christening of my sister Tate's son. I've agreed to be his godfather. I thought you might like to come with me."

Belinda wasn't sure what to think, what to do. "That's two months from now. Maybe the ranch will sell, and you'll be long gone by then."

"Maybe. Maybe not."

"I couldn't leave Madelyn alone," Belinda said.

"I've already invited Maddy to come, and she's agreed."

"Maddy's your grandmother. She has a reason to come."

"I want you to come, Belinda."

Belinda searched Faron's face. "Why?"

"Because this will be an important moment in my life, Princess. And I want to share it with you."

"I..."

"You don't have to answer me now. Just think about it."

A moment later Belinda was alone. Faron had disappeared in the direction of the barn.

Over the next month Faron kept his distance from her. At first Belinda was grateful. She figured he stayed away so she wouldn't feel pressured to accept his invitation. It also allowed her to avoid having to examine her feelings for the Cowboy. However, Belinda soon realized that unless she spent time with Faron, she wouldn't have a chance to find out whether she wanted their relationship to develop further.

So when she got a call from a corporate buyer who wanted to take a look at King's Castle, she saddled her horse and went in search of Faron. She found him working on another windmill on the northern border of the ranch.

"I thought you had hired men to do the manual labor," she said as she stepped down from the saddle.

"This just needed a little fine-tuning. Thought I'd take care of it myself."

Belinda took a moment to admire the man. He had removed his shirt, and his bronzed upper torso glistened with sweat. The muscles in his back bunched as he manhandled the wrench he was holding. He twisted it once more, then stood and threw the wrench into the tool box in the back of his pickup. He pulled a bandanna out of his back jeans pocket and used it to wipe the sweat from his brow.

He seemed to realize suddenly that she was staring at him. Only this time when he met her gaze, she didn't look away. She did nothing to hide her desire. Nothing could have been a more powerful aphrodisiac.

"Why did you come out here?" he asked.

"There was a phone call..." Belinda lost her train of thought as Faron reached out and cupped her cheek with the palm of his hand. He tilted her face up and it seemed the most natural thing in the world to lift her lips to meet his.

Warm. Welcome. Like coming home. She hadn't known she needed his kiss so much.

Soft. Receptive. She belonged to him. He must have been insane to have stayed away so long.

Faron pulled her into his arms, nearly crushing her with the strength of his embrace. He spread his legs and settled her in the cradle of his thighs.

Belinda wondered if this was what it felt like to be in love. She couldn't deny the passion that flared between the two of them whenever they were together. Touching Faron gave her as much pleasure as having him touch her.

It had been too long for both of them. He was impatient, but so was she. Once Faron had her breasts bare under the sunlight, he took his time. He bent his head to kiss her soft curves and then suckled her. Belinda arched into his caresses, and her traitorous knees once more gave way.

Faron picked her up in his arms, but the only shady spot available was already occupied by cattle.

"How about going for a ride?"

He set her back in the saddle, then mounted behind her. When Belinda started to rebutton her blouse, Faron stopped her.

"Don't. I want to hold you while we're riding." Belinda leaned back into his embrace, and Faron's hands crossed around her, cupping her breasts. Faron kicked the palomino into a lope, heading toward the river and the cottonwoods he knew they would find there.

It was the most decadent ride Belinda had ever taken. By the time they got to the river, each of them had aroused the other beyond bearing. Faron slid off the palomino's back and pulled Belinda down onto the ground. He had them both stripped in record time.

The day was hot, but the grass was cool on Belinda's naked backside. Their coupling was urgent, so quick that each offered a quite unnecessary apology to the other.

"I should have waited—"

"I couldn't wait—"

They both laughed, and then hugged each other and rolled to their sides, their bodies still joined. They lay like that a long time, until at last they separated to lie on their backs and stare at the sky through the rustling leaves of the cottonwood.

"So why did you come out to see me?" Faron asked as he nibbled on the lobe of her ear.

"We got a call from a corporate buyer. He wants to take a look at King's Castle." Belinda was close enough to be aware of the way Faron stiffened. It was still a month until Labor Day.

"When does he want to come?"

"Tomorrow."

So soon. Faron wasn't ready to leave King's Castle yet. Over the past month he had begun to see the potential of the place. With a little better management it could become a successful enterprise again. Of course, a woman alone would have a tough time managing, but a couple—a couple could do just fine.

He didn't dare mention to Belinda what he was thinking. She couldn't even make up her mind to take a trip to Texas with him. How could he expect her to consider marriage and a life spent together at King's Castle?

Faron surprised himself with how easily that thought had formed in his mind. Was he really ready to get married? What would his family say when they heard he wanted to marry his stepmother? He could hear Garth now. His eldest brother would think Faron had lost his mind.

But Faron knew if his family met Belinda, they would understand how he had fallen in love with her. Which was why he had to convince her to come to the christening at Hawk's Way on Labor Day.

Now that they knew he had a different father, he wanted them to see that he wasn't going to allow his bastardy to separate him from his family. In fact, he wanted them to see that he had merely extended his family to include his grandmother. He hadn't figured out yet what he would say about Belinda.

"Did you tell the buyer we'd be glad to show him around?" he asked her.

"I told him we'd call him back."

Faron arched a brow. "Was there some reason you wanted to wait?"

"I just thought... what if he makes us an offer?"

"If it's a reasonable offer, we'll accept."

"Do you really want to sell the ranch?"

"Don't you?" Faron asked.

"I guess I do," Belinda said. "But it's been home for a long time. It'll seem strange to live in town."

"Is that what you'd do? Move to town?"

"Where else would I go?"

Home with me to Hawk's Way. But Faron didn't say what he was thinking. It was too soon to tell Belinda the plans he had for the two of them. He didn't want to scare her away.

It wasn't until she had told the story about spending the night with a brown-eyed, redheaded steer that he had realized just how limited her experience with men was. He knew she'd had a bad time with Wayne Prescott. He could understand her reluctance to trust another man.

But if he'd thought his time was short before, it was down to nothing now. Tomorrow. It might all end tomorrow if the buyer made an offer they couldn't refuse. So maybe he should say something to her now, let her know that he didn't intend ever to let her go.

Faron opened his mouth to declare his love and shut it again.

Belinda was asleep.

He lay down beside her and pulled her into his arms. Tomorrow would be soon enough to speak his mind. Maybe the buyer wouldn't want the property. Maybe there would be no decisions to be made right away. He would just wait and see.

Seven

"How dare you refuse an offer for this ranch without consulting me!" Belinda raged.

"He offered a quarter of what the place was worth!" Faron retorted.

"I don't care how much he offered. What I care about is the fact that you made the decision without saying anything to me. I should have been consulted."

"Both of us have to agree for this place to get sold. Since I would have refused the offer anyway, it didn't make sense to get you involved."

"Didn't make sense? I can't believe what I'm hearing! That's just the sort of thing Wayne would have said. 'No sense troubling your pretty little head with business.' I own half of King's Castle, and by God, I'll be a part of any decisions that are made regarding this ranch.''

Faron realized he had made a big mistake, and he quickly sought to make amends. "I'm sorry. Next time—''

"If there is a next time!" Belinda put her fisted hands on her hips. "There aren't so many corporate buyers out there that we can afford to refuse an honest offer.''

"So maybe we just won't sell!''

"Right! And when the bank comes to collect the mortgage payment what do you suggest we use for money?''

"I've got—''

"I don't want to rely on you to keep this place afloat.''

"Why not?" Faron asked.

"I learned how much that sort of debt can cost when I was married to your father!''

There it was again. The comparison of Faron with his father, and it hadn't been a compliment. "I am not my father,'' he said quietly.

"Could have fooled me,'' Belinda muttered. "Tyrannical, autocratic—''

"That's enough,'' Faron said. "I get your point.''

Belinda was still quivering with rage. And fighting tears. She had talked herself into believing that

Faron was different from his father. His actions today, discounting her opinion and involvement in a way similar to what Wayne might have done, was a deep disappointment. Her romantic bubble had burst, and she was sharply, brutally disillusioned.

"I hope you're not going to use this incident as an excuse not to come to Texas," Faron said.

"I've learned never to make decisions when I'm angry," Belinda admitted. "Maybe when I've calmed down we can talk about where we go from here."

She turned on her heel and left Faron standing alone in Wayne's study. He leaned back in the swivel chair and put his boot heels up on the roll-top desk.

Was what he had done so wrong? Faron was used to making decisions on his own. Except on major issues that concerned Hawk's Way. Then he and Garth would discuss the matter... As he should have discussed the matter with Belinda, Faron realized.

If the situation had been reversed, he would have been furious if Belinda had made a major decision regarding King's Castle without him. She deserved no less consideration than he would have demanded for himself. Unconsciously he had put himself in the role of caretaker, but it was clear now, if it hadn't been before, that Belinda intended to be nothing less than an equal partner.

Which he was willing to be. Only what he wanted from her was not just a business partnership, but a deeply committed personal relationship.

Faron cursed the father who had so wounded the woman he loved. His recent error hadn't helped matters. Belinda was sure to be less trusting of him in the future. It was going to be a challenge convincing her that she didn't have to worry about repeating the mistakes with him that she had made with his father.

Meanwhile Belinda had retreated to the vegetable garden behind the house where she was on her hands and knees pulling up weeds between a row of snap beans and a row of tomatoes. She wasn't precisely aware when Madelyn joined her. The older woman wore a floppy hat to keep the sun off and gloves to protect her hands. The two women worked in silence for a while, as they had on many another day. It was Madelyn who finally spoke.

"You're going to get sunstroke working without a hat."

"Don't you start treating me like a child. I get enough of that from Faron."

"Oh?"

"He turned down an offer for the ranch without even consulting me. Just like Wayne, he—"

Madelyn's interruption cut off Belinda's tirade before it even got started. "Oh, no, my dear. He's not like Wayne at all."

"It didn't even cross his mind to speak to me before—"

"But he apologized when you pointed out his mistake, didn't he?"

"Yes, but—"

"Wayne would never have apologized. I think you should give Faron the benefit of the doubt."

Belinda dusted the dirt off her hands. "Does that mean you also think I should go to Texas with him?"

"Tell me one good reason why you shouldn't go."

"I've never been beyond the borders of Wyoming in my entire life."

"Land sakes, girl. All the more reason to go."

"I've never been on an airplane."

"Flying is a piece of cake."

Belinda resorted to the real reasons she had reservations about going to Texas. "I'm the widow of the man with whom Faron's mother had an affair. I'm Faron's stepmother."

"When the Whitelaws meet you they'll be just as fond of you as Faron is."

"Faron isn't—"

Madelyn pursed her lips and looked at Belinda across the row of snap beans. "Don't try to deny it. I've got eyes, Belinda, and I'm not too old to see what's right in front of my nose."

Belinda pulled a snap bean and broke it into pieces looking for the tiny beans inside.

Madelyn reached out and put a hand on Belinda's knee. "You're like my very own daughter, Belinda. I only want you to be happy. I think Faron could make you happy."

"If I go to the christening with Faron, it doesn't mean I'm committing myself to anything where he's concerned. I want to be sure you understand that and don't get your hopes up."

"Of course not, dear. I understand perfectly. It would just be a much-needed break from all the work here. A chance for you to get away and see another part of the country."

"That's all I'd be doing," Belinda affirmed.

A few weeks later, when she found herself facing the Whitelaws' antebellum mansion at Hawk's Way, Belinda was having second thoughts. The ranch house was an imposing two-story white frame structure with four twenty-foot-high fluted columns and railed first- and second-story porches. The road leading to the house was lined with majestic magnolias. The branches of a moss-laden live oak draped the roof of the house. It had a majesty every bit as profound as The Castle.

Faron had one arm around her shoulder and the other arm around Madelyn as he escorted them up the front steps and inside the foyer. "This is my home," he told Belinda.

She could hear the pride in his voice. The reason for it was evident in the well-kept, homey furnishings she found inside. There was tradition in this house, oak and pine furniture that had survived the rough and tumble of generations of Whitelaw sons and daughters. An ancient map framed over the mantel delineated what had once been the vast reaches of Hawk's Way in the Texas panhandle.

"It's beautiful," she said. "You must have missed being here these past few months."

Faron was surprised to realize that he hadn't missed Hawk's Way as much as he might have expected to when he left. The reason was obvious. In Wyoming he had found something to fill the hole inside him. He no longer felt the same sense of belonging here since he had staked his claim on his father's land—and his father's wife.

Faron's brothers and sister were arrayed in the parlor with their families. The two babies, Jesse and Honey's daughter and Adam and Tate's son, were sleeping in small antique cribs. From descriptions Faron had given her, Belinda easily recognized the two couples. Honey was sitting in Jesse's lap on a chair in front of the fireplace. Adam and Tate were sitting close beside each other on the couch.

Garth was standing with an arm resting on the thick pine mantel above the stone fireplace. There was another young woman in the room, but Belinda couldn't imagine who she could be.

Faron proudly introduced Belinda and Madelyn to the assembled group. "This is my grandmother, Madelyn Prescott," he said. "I call her Maddy."

There was an awkward moment when Belinda wondered whether Faron's family would accept the old woman. Tate made the first move. She jumped up from the couch and crossed with her hands extended to the older woman. "It's so nice to meet you, Maddy." She gave Maddy a quick, hard hug. Then she stood back and looked to see whether her brother resembled his grandmother. "Oh, my goodness. Faron has your eyes! Come see, Jesse, Garth."

The two large men came forward to greet the old woman and to agree with Tate that yes, Faron and Maddy had eyes the same unique gray green color. Honey and Adam soon joined them and everyone began talking a mile a minute.

In the confusion Belinda was tempted to sneak back out the way she had come. Just when she thought Faron had forgotten all about her, he raised his hand for quiet. It took a few moments for the commotion to die down.

You could have heard a pin drop when he said, "And this is Belinda Prescott, my stepmother."

"That's the ugly stepmother?" Jesse whispered. His wife elbowed him in the ribs to shut him up.

It was Garth who took control of what could have become a very awkward situation. "I'm pleased to meet you, Belinda."

But Belinda didn't think he was at all pleased. She didn't know when she had ever met such a granite-faced man. His greeting was formal and his manner stiff. Belinda felt like crying. She didn't belong here. She wasn't part of this family in any way, shape or form. When she would have turned and run, a beautiful young woman with long blond hair and widely spaced gray eyes reached out and grasped her hand.

"Hi. I'm Candice—Candy Baylor. I guess you and I are the only two people here who aren't family."

Candy smiled, and Belinda immediately felt better.

"I've been working at Hawk's Way this summer, and I can imagine how you must feel, meeting this rowdy bunch for the first time."

"They are a little overwhelming," Belinda conceded.

"I don't know if you remember me," Faron said, extending a hand to Candy. "I'm Faron." Faron shot a look at Garth as though to say "What's she doing here?" But Garth's face remained stony.

"Of course I remember you," Candy said. "Last time I was here with my father you yanked my braids at the breakfast table."

Faron grinned. "Guilty. Was that only three years ago? You've grown up a little since then."

Garth interrupted, saying, "I think it's time you showed Maddy and Belinda where they'll be staying."

Faron was intrigued by Garth's possessive attitude toward Candy. That was a situation he intended to find out more about later. "Come on upstairs, ladies, and I'll show you to your rooms."

After taking Maddy to her room, Faron led Belinda to hers.

Belinda was relieved to see that she and Maddy were staying on a wing of the house that was separated from the rest of the family. She felt less pleased when she saw that Faron had settled Maddy in a room that was at the opposite end of the hall from hers. She looked at the room next to hers and said, "Who sleeps there?"

"I do," Faron answered.

Belinda turned startled violet eyes on him. "I thought the family was on a separate wing."

"The rest of them are."

Belinda stared at him for a moment. "Faron—"

He leaned over and gave her a quick, hard kiss. "Don't ask me to move you somewhere else, Princess. I want you close to me."

He didn't plead, he didn't cajole. Just that simple request. Belinda remembered Fiona's advice. And what Madelyn had said. It was time to act on her feelings for the Cowboy. Time to take a chance. "All right," she said at last. "I'll stay here."

She heard his exhaled sigh of relief and smiled inwardly. So, he wasn't as confident as he had led her to believe. Somehow that made her feel better. "Do you suppose there's something I can do to help with supper?"

"As soon as you finish unpacking, come on downstairs to the kitchen, and I'm sure Charlie will put you to work."

"I can't wait to meet the man who taught you how to stack a dishwasher," Belinda said with a grin.

Faron kissed her again, then turned and left her. If he didn't go now, he was afraid he wouldn't go at all.

The chaos in the kitchen seemed familiar to Belinda, who had so recently been visited by her siblings and their families. Everyone was there pitching in to get things on the table except Garth and Candy, who had headed for the barn to check on a mare that was expected to foal in the next day or so.

Belinda was amazed and amused at the contrast between Faron's family and her own. Maybe it was because she had sisters, but there seemed to be a lot more roughhousing among Faron's clan. Even Tate, Faron's youngest sister, could hold her own with her brothers. When Faron threw a handful of potato peelings at her, she responded by throwing an entire peeled potato back at him.

Faron simply caught the potato and tossed it to Jesse, who tossed it to Honey, who tossed it to Adam, who tossed it back to Tate. She handed it primly to Charlie One-Horse, who cut it into four pieces and dumped it into the pot of boiling water on the stove. Belinda didn't know when she'd had so much fun making a meal.

It was harder for Belinda to cope with her feelings when she watched Honey and Tate nursing their babies after supper. They sat in the parlor, a blanket thrown over their shoulders in deference to her presence, and suckled their children in full view of the Whitelaw men and Tate's husband, Adam. As though it was the most normal thing in the world for two nursing mothers to be sitting in a roomful of cowboys.

And it was.

Belinda's chest ached with the feelings that assailed her. She met Faron's eyes across the room. For the first time in eight years, Belinda allowed herself to imagine what her life might have been like if she had waited to fall in love and marry. It was a wonderful picture, full of love and laughter . . . and children.

Suddenly she couldn't stay any longer. She rose as quietly as she could and left the parlor, heading upstairs. She felt, as much as heard, Faron coming up the stairs behind her. She pretended she didn't know he was there, just kept putting one foot in front of the other until she reached her bedroom.

Just as Faron caught up to her she stepped inside her bedroom and closed the door behind her.

She leaned back against the door, closed her eyes and listened. She could hear him breathing on the other side of the door.

"Princess," he whispered. "Are you all right?"

"I'm fine," she whispered back. "Good night, Cowboy."

She could almost feel the tension on the other side of the wooden panel. She had known what memories it would conjure if she called him Cowboy. She felt her body rouse as she remembered their lovemaking.

"Princess." His voice was hoarse. "Open the door."

She turned and pressed her forehead against the cool painted surface. Her hand was on the knob. She would have turned it, except she heard Maddy call to him.

"Is Belinda all right?"

"She's fine, Maddy. Just a little tired, I think."

"I'm a little tired myself. Good night, Faron."

"Good night, Maddy."

Belinda waited and listened. A moment later she opened the door. But Faron was gone.

I should have opened the door right away, as soon as he called. I should have invited him inside. I want him here with me. I don't want to be alone tonight.

All she had to do was go downstairs and find him. All she had to do...

Belinda stripped and found her nightgown. But she didn't put it on. Instead, she slipped naked between the sheets. And dreamed of a certain cowboy making love to a woman he called Princess.

She must have been more tired than she had thought, because the next thing she knew, Faron was knocking on the connecting door between their rooms.

The connecting door!

Belinda scrambled into a sitting position on the four-poster bed and clutched the sheets to her naked body as the door opened and Faron stuck his head inside.

"When I didn't hear anything moving in here I thought I'd better make sure you were awake. The convoy to the church leaves in about an hour."

"I can't believe you put us in *connecting* rooms!" Belinda said.

The sheet slipped on one side as she clutched it tighter, and Faron was treated to a glimpse of a pink aureole. I've made no secret how I feel about you, Princess."

"What will your family think?"

"My family will mind their own business."

A call from downstairs drifted across the tense silence between them.

"Faaaarrrooon! You're eggs are done," Tate yelled.

"See you at breakfast, Princess." He grinned and pulled the connecting door closed just before the pillow Belinda had thrown landed against it.

If Belinda had thought the Whitelaws would act any more civilized at breakfast than they had at supper, she was sadly mistaken.

There was raw egg dripping down the front of the refrigerator, and the shell lay cracked and broken on a red tile floor dusted with a fine layer of flour. To her chagrin she realized she was sorry she hadn't been a part of the juvenile food fight.

"Coffee?" Tate asked as Belinda stepped into the kitchen.

"Yes, thanks."

"You look absolutely gorgeous!" Tate said.

Belinda froze as every male eye in the room turned to stare at her. She had put her hair up in an elegant twist and was wearing a sheath that outlined her figure, even though it concealed her from neck to knee.

Faron was surprised at the surge of protectiveness that arose when Belinda became the object of all eyes. He slipped an arm around her waist and said, "And she's as nice as she is beautiful."

The warning was there. Unspoken but irrefutable. *She's mine and I protect what's mine.*

It was Charlie One-Horse who diffused the tension in the room. He walked over to Maddy and said, "I 'spect I gotta vote that this here is the purtiest woman in the room."

Maddy blushed prettily and for a moment the glow in her eyes made her look exceedingly lovely.

Not to be outdone, Jesse announced that Honey was the sweetest in the room, and Adam countered that Tate was without a doubt the cutest one there. Until the only woman in the room who hadn't been complimented was Candy Baylor.

She stood by the stove, spatula in hand, staring at Garth and waiting.

But he offered not a word of praise to the young woman. At last he turned to Tate and said, "We'd better get moving if we're going to be on time. I'll go get the car."

He turned on his heel and stalked out the screen door, letting it slam behind him.

Candy's face paled as she stared after him.

There was a moment of awful silence before Belinda said, "It's hard to tell which needs a dipping worse, him or the floor of this kitchen."

Faron was at first stunned that Belinda would take on his eldest brother and then amused by the way she had chosen to do it. His grin soon found company, and the tension eased as everyone finished their breakfasts and divided into groups for the trip to church.

Belinda noticed that Candy avoided going in Garth's car, and she couldn't blame the woman. It wasn't until Garth had refused to play the game this morning that she had realized there was more going on between the couple than met the eye.

The christening was held before the church service began. Belinda sat in the first pew with Candy, Madelyn and the rest of the Whitelaw family. Faron stood beside his sister, Tate, and held her son, Brett, in his arms.

Belinda overheard Faron speaking to Tate as she handed the baby into his care.

"Thanks, Tate, for wanting me to be Brett's godfather even though—"

Tate had hugged him fiercely, the baby caught between them. "You're my brother, and I love you. Nothing—*nothing*—is going to change that."

Faron's eyes were moist when Tate let go of him.

Belinda was sitting at an angle where she could see Faron when he stood before the church altar. The love there, the exquisite tenderness on his face as he looked down on the child in his arms, moved her to tears. She listened as Faron promised to stand in the stead of the baby's parents in the event it was necessary, to be godfather to Brett Patrick Philips.

After the church service, the Whitelaw family was surprisingly subdued, perhaps awed by the dignity of the christening ceremony, as Belinda had been herself. But the celebration that afternoon, a picnic in the backyard under a spreading live oak, was as rowdy as any drunken brawl she had seen in the diner where she had worked in Casper. Only none of them was drinking anything stronger than ice tea.

"Having fun?" Faron asked, when he caught up to her halfway through the afternoon. She was dressed in cutoffs, a T-shirt and tennis shoes. Her hair was in a ponytail. She looked about fifteen, and he felt like a teenager with the biggest crush of his life.

She grinned and threw a Frisbee at him. "I'm having a ball!"

Faron caught it and pitched it back to her. They played for a while until Faron threw the Frisbee as far as he could beyond the crowd. When Belinda ran after it, he ran after her. When he caught her, he picked her up and threw her over his shoulder.

"Where are we going?" Belinda asked with a breathless laugh.

Faron didn't answer, just kept on walking.

"Faron? Put me down, Faron." Belinda started wriggling on Faron's shoulder, but he grabbed her legs and pinned her against him.

As soon as Faron entered the barn, Belinda knew where she was. It was dark and cool inside. It smelled of horses and hay and the pungent odor of manure. A horse nickered from one of the stalls. Faron carried her to an empty stall and shifted her off his shoulder until she was standing in front of him.

"Here we are," he said.

Belinda just stared at him. Her heart was pounding with excitement. All she did was take one step toward him and Faron gathered her close in his arms. He lifted her legs and wrapped them around him. She clutched at his shoulders and buried her face at his throat.

"You feel so good, Princess."

Faron backed her up against the stall and found her breasts through the T-shirt with his mouth.

"Faron? Are you in here?"

"Damn, damn, damn," Faron muttered. "What do you want, Garth?"

"Candy will be here in a minute to check on that foaling mare."

He had forgotten about the mare. "All right. Thanks."

Belinda was too caught up in the passion of the moment to realize they had been interrupted. Faron unwound her legs from around him and tried to stand her up, but her knees wouldn't support her. He picked her up in his arms and headed out of the barn. Garth had conveniently, considerately disappeared.

Belinda hid her face against Faron's shoulder. "Looks like our timing was a little off," she mumbled.

"Don't I know it," Faron muttered.

"Hey, you two!" Tate called. "We're going to play a game of softball. You want in?"

Faron looked down and met Belinda's rueful look. "Sure. We'll join you."

They spent the rest of the afternoon in a game of softball, then tossed the Frisbee again until it started to get dark. Madelyn kept an eye on the babies and generally supervised activities.

As they were clearing away the picnic table, Belinda watched the various couples begin to pair off. Again, her eyes sought out Faron. He was walking toward her. She felt her belly tighten as he stalked her. She stood and waited for him to come to her. He didn't stop when he passed by her, merely paused long enough to whisper in her ear.

Belinda shivered when he said, "Tonight."

Eight

Faron was in the kitchen, waiting for the house to get quiet, waiting for the right moment to go to Belinda. He hadn't *asked* if he could come to her, he had *told* her he was coming. He wished he could know for sure that when he knocked on her door this time, his Princess would let him in.

"What are you doing down here so late?"

Faron turned and found himself confronted by Charlie One-Horse. The half-Indian codger was more than a hired hand. He had been part father, part mother and longtime friend to the Whitelaws. He had been a source of wisdom and knowledge all of Faron's life.

"Female problems," Charlie muttered.

Faron's lips curled in the semblance of a smile. "How did you know?"

"Only reason a man wanders the house at night instead of going to bed where he belongs." Charlie concentrated on retying the beaded rawhide thong on one of his black braids so Faron wouldn't see the concern in his eyes.

"As long as you're here, I could use some advice," Faron said.

"I'm listenin'." Charlie crossed to the refrigerator, opened the door and stood there looking inside.

"I'm in love with Belinda Prescott."

"So? What's the problem?"

"Her first marriage—her marriage to my father—was a disaster. I don't know if she's ever going to let another man get close to her."

Charlie took out a container of strawberries and set it on the counter. He got a fork from the drawer, then stood at the counter eating the ripe red berries. "Time is the best salve to heal wounds of the heart."

"I don't have a lot of time," Faron said in a tormented voice.

Charlie One-Horse forked a huge strawberry and held it up so he could examine it. It was a "double," a strawberry that should have been two and had ended up one. "You'll just have to be patient. Show her that you love her. Once she realizes what love is supposed to be, she'll come to you like a filly to a hand outstretched with sugar." He stuffed the strawberry into his mouth and began munching.

Faron couldn't deny Charlie had given him good advice. But it seemed too little, too late. He could feel time running out. Tomorrow they would be headed back to King's Castle. Next time a corporate buyer showed up, he might not be so lucky. Next time the man might make an offer he couldn't—and Belinda wouldn't—refuse.

Faron crossed the room and laid a hand on Charlie's shoulder. "Thanks, Charlie. Good night."

Charlie just grunted because his mouth was too full of strawberries for him to speak.

Faron headed for the stairs, then detoured to the parlor. He wasn't quite ready yet to face Belinda's possible rejection. He slumped down into his regular chair in front of the fireplace, thinking he was alone, only to discover that Garth was there before him.

"What are you doing sitting in the dark?" Faron asked.

"I could ask you the same thing," Garth responded.

Neither man gave a reason why he was there. Neither needed to. As Charlie had noted, only a woman kept a man from his bed when he ought to be sleeping. They sat there staring into a fire that was no more than glowing embers. Occasionally

Garth drank from a glass of whiskey he held in one hand.

"Did you find the peace of mind you were looking for when you set out for Wyoming?" Garth asked at last.

"It was worth the trip to find Maddy," Faron said. "She's a feisty old broad." Faron thrust his hands through his hair and tried to smooth it back down again. "And I love the land, King's Castle. I don't know how to explain it. It's so different from the canyons and gullies on Hawk's Way. There's something about those endless rolling green prairies that feeds my soul. I'm going to miss it when it's sold."

"So don't sell."

"What?"

"Don't sell the place. Keep it."

"Belinda Prescott might have a few words to say about that. She wants to move into town."

"So let her go. Buy her half of the place from her."

"I—" Faron didn't know how to explain to his brother that a great deal of what he found so captivating about King's Castle was the fact that Belinda Prescott lived there.

Garth shrugged when Faron made no effort to explain himself further. "It was just an idea. So what did you find out about Wayne Prescott?"

"He wasn't a very noble character, my father."

"You knew that before you left," Garth pointed out.

"He abused Belinda."

"I'm sorry to hear that."

It was the first time Faron had ever heard Garth utter those words. It brought a lump to his throat to realize that his brother understood Faron's anger and frustration without him having to say more.

"I don't have to ask if you love her," Garth said. "It's written all over your face when you look at her. Are you sure you're doing the right thing to get involved with her?"

Trust Garth to go right to the heart of the problem. "It's right for me. I'm not so sure about how she feels."

"Does it bother you at all that she was Wayne Prescott's wife?" Garth asked curiously.

Faron took time to seriously consider Garth's question. At last he said, "Only because he treated her badly."

"So what are you doing down here? I never thought you were a coward."

Faron took enough umbrage to say, "I'm not the only Whitelaw sitting alone in the dark. What's the story between you and Candy Baylor?"

"None of your business," Garth said brusquely.

A slow smile grew on Faron's face. "Well, well, big brother. How the mighty have fallen."

"What's that supposed to mean?"

"You figure it out. I'm going upstairs where I hope there's a lady waiting for me. You can sit here alone in the dark all night if you want. But I suspect there might be a lady somewhere waiting for you, too."

"She'll have a long wait," Garth retorted.

Faron laughed. "Good night, Garth. Sleep well."

"Get out of here and leave me in peace."

"I'll leave, but I doubt you'll have much peace until you seek out a certain blond-haired, gray-eyed woman."

Faron had just reached the doorway when he heard the loud splintering of glass against the stone fireplace. He was almost sorry he would be leaving tomorrow. He would give his eyeteeth to be around to see his cynical, misogynistic brother finally fall in love with a woman.

As he climbed the stairs, Faron was aware of the silence in the house. When he reached Belinda's door he knocked and then turned the knob. It was open, and he let himself in.

There was a light on beside the bed. Belinda wasn't there.

"Damn." He should have known she wasn't ready yet to hear what he wanted to say to her. He shouldn't have pushed so hard. He had frightened her so badly she had run. But where the hell had she gone?

Faron felt like throwing something. He settled for slamming one fisted hand into the palm of the other. He clenched his back teeth and stared out the window into the distance. He would just have to take Charlie One-Horse's advice and be patient. Belinda couldn't go far. And he would be here waiting when she returned.

Faron crossed to the connecting door between the two bedrooms and yanked it open. He stomped across the threshold and stopped short. His jaw fell agape.

There, sound asleep in his bed, lay his golden Princess. She was wearing a filmy nightgown with a delicate lace trim that cupped her breasts. Her hand pillowed her head and one knee was drawn up so that the nightgown revealed the length of her from her toes to the top of her hip.

He sat down carefully beside her on the brass bed, but even that slight movement woke her. She turned lazily onto her back and looked up at him through half-closed eyes.

"Hi," she said. "I've been waiting for you."

Faron's heart began to gallop. "I'm glad you're here."

Belinda slipped a hand around Faron's nape and drew his mouth down to hers. Just before their lips met she said, "I like your family, Faron. I wish..."

"What do you wish, Princess?"

"I wish I had waited . . . to find you."

"I'm here now, Princess. And I'm not going anywhere."

Belinda took the initiative in their lovemaking. Faron made it easy for her. He responded to the barest touch of her fingertips. It was as though he could sense what she needed, what she desired. She urged his mouth down to hers. The kiss was gentle at first, tentative, but Belinda's need was great, and there was an answering fire in the Cowboy.

Faron encouraged her by showing her how much pleasure he found in her kisses, in her touch. She found his leashed passion as seductive as an aphrodisiac. She slowly undressed him, one piece of clothing at a time, indulging her need to feel the textures of his body. The crisp hair on his chest. The hardness of muscle and sinew. The petal softness of his eyelids and the shell of his ears.

"Take off your nightgown, Princess."

Belinda hesitated a moment, then reached down and pulled it up over her head. Finally she was as naked as he was. His eyes adored her. Then his hands and mouth followed where his gaze led. Where Belinda touched him, he touched her. Shoulders. Ribs. Stomach. Hips. Buttocks.

Faron hadn't known he could find such pleasure with a woman. He wanted desperately to speak of his love. But he knew he must be patient. He had to wait until she was ready to hear the words. He had to show her that he loved her, so there could be no doubt in her mind how he felt. She had to know that he would cherish her. That he would never abuse her as his father had.

Faron's body tensed as Belinda's hands surrounded him and urged him close. Her hips rose and he impaled her. They rolled once and she was above him, her hair a cloak that tantalized him by half hiding her breasts.

Belinda felt free to love Faron in ways she had never loved her husband. She had an unbelievable sense of her own feminine power as she caressed him. His eyes glowed with the warmth of his need and desire. Her body tightened in response to his guttural groans of pleasure. His urgent kisses made her feel wanted and loved.

He rolled her under him once more, mantling her body with his own. "Come with me, Princess. Reach for the stars."

Belinda did. She reached for the happiness she had never allowed herself to even dream of having. She let down the barriers she had put up to keep herself safe from a man to whom she had been a possession. And allowed herself to love a man who treasured her because of who she was.

Faron caught Belinda's cries of exultation with his mouth. He revered her with his hands, with his mouth, with his body. He brought her to the pinnacle, and they rose beyond it together.

Faron wasn't expecting the tears. "Princess? What's wrong? Did I hurt you? Are you all right?"

"I'm fine," she managed through a throat that was constricted so much it prevented easy speech.

"I don't know why I'm crying. You were wonderful. It was wonderful."

He gathered her in his arms and held her while she cried. Belinda had a pretty good idea what was causing the lump in her throat. It was the pain of knowledge. Of regret for the years she had foolishly wasted. It was fear of the course she was determined to embark upon. And hope for the future.

Because now she could no longer deny to herself what she felt. She was in love with Faron Whitelaw.

That should have been the end of the fairy tale, and the beginning of the rest of her life. She would simply accept the handsome cowboy's proposal and they would live happily ever after.

Only the Cowboy hadn't proposed. He hadn't even said those three little words, "I love you."

Eventually the constriction in her throat eased. She grabbed a sheet and dabbed at the corners of her eyes. "Faron?"

"Hmm."

"I'm sorry for falling apart on you like that."

"Can you tell me about it?"

"I..." Belinda should have been able to tell Faron that she loved him. That she was hoping they would spend the rest of their lives together. But memories of times when Wayne had taken her tenderest emotions and ridiculed them came to mind. And kept her silent.

It was one thing to say she was going to forget the past and go on with her life. It was quite another to be able to do it. Apparently the wounds were deeper than she had believed. It might take a little longer for them to heal completely. "It's nothing you did, Faron," she said at last.

"Was it something my father did?"

Belinda's hand played across Faron's chest, winding in the black curls that arrowed downward toward his navel. Her fingertips skimmed across a male nipple, and she watched in fascination as it peaked. "I don't want to talk about Wayne. I want to make love to you."

Her fingertips skimmed down the front of him until she cupped him in her hand. His response was immediate and totally gratifying. Belinda grinned. "My, my, Cowboy. What have we here?"

"Don't play with fire, Princess, unless you're ready for the heat."

Belinda's laugh was cut short when Faron's hand slid down the front of her in imitation of her own intimate exploration. He slipped a finger inside her, then another, and Belinda arched up as his thumb sought out the sensitive nubbin that was the source of her desire.

Faron's mouth caught the cries of passion as Belinda arched up under his provocative caresses. But she would never again be a passive partner. She sought out the places on Faron's body that she knew drove him wild. The crease at his thigh, the dimples above his buttocks, the point where taut belly slid into crisp curls.

They taunted each other, refusing to be the first to give in to the sensual teasing. They laughed when they had the breath to do so. They kissed, their tongues entwining, their teeth nipping tender flesh.

And they loved. With their hearts. With their souls. With their whole beings.

But he never said, "I love you."

Neither did she.

When the sun dawned and sent the first rays of light across the tangled sheets, they were still wrapped in each other's arms. Neither wanted the fairy tale to end.

A knock on the door sent Belinda searching for her nightgown. Faron slipped on his jeans and buttoned them halfway.

"We don't have anything to hide," Faron said.

"What if it's Madelyn?" Belinda hissed. "I don't—I'm not ready to face her like this." She yanked her nightgown on, then raced for the door between the two rooms.

She was halfway there when Faron caught her and swung her back into his arms. He kissed her hard. "We have to talk, Princess."

"Later. Let me go, Faron. Please."

He let her go and she disappeared, closing the door silently behind her. Faron answered the persistent knock and found Garth at the door.

"This better be important," Faron growled.

"I thought it was. There was a call on the office phone. Somebody wants to buy King's Castle, but he needs to take a look at it tomorrow. Here's the number where you can reach him."

Faron grimaced. "All right. I'll be right down."

Garth took a look at the disheveled state of the bed and arched a brow. "Take your time, little brother. Take all the time you need."

Before Faron could protest, Garth was gone.

A second later Belinda was back in Faron's room. "Who was it?"

"Garth."

"What did he want?"

"A corporate buyer tracked us down. He wants to take a look at King's Castle—tomorrow."

Belinda sank down onto the bed. "What are we going to do?"

"*We* are going to listen to his offer."

Faron's reference to the fact it would be a joint decision wasn't lost on Belinda. "I...I suppose we should."

"Then we'll have to make a decision whether or not to sell."

The last thing Belinda wanted to contemplate right now was the sale of the ranch. Because once it was sold, Faron would be returning to Hawk's Way. Now that she had seen it, she knew there was no way Faron could prefer King's Castle to the comforts to be found here.

Furthermore, his family lived in Texas. She had seen how close Faron was to his brothers and sister. Family was important to him. Faron couldn't possibly contemplate living the rest of his life in Wyoming, separated from his family except for visits on holidays. Belinda knew how hard that was, and she wouldn't wish it on anyone.

Belinda tried to imagine Faron offering to bring her back to Hawk's Way as his wife. Naturally, Madelyn would have to be part of the package. However, Belinda couldn't imagine Garth Whitelaw accepting Wayne Prescott's mother into his household. And she could never abandon Madelyn. Which meant Belinda could never live here, either.

"I'll meet you downstairs after you've had a chance to get dressed," Faron said. "And we'll give this guy a call."

"All right," Belinda said.

But when Faron tried to draw her into his arms she stepped back. "I need to get dressed," she said. She turned from him and walked away.

Faron didn't know what had gone wrong, but he had a pretty good idea it had to do with selling the ranch. But he would be damned if he could figure out whether his Princess wanted the place sold—or not.

Nine

It was a toss-up who heaved the bigger sigh of relief when the corporate buyer made a ridiculously low offer. Faron tried to look disappointed. Belinda matched him furrow for furrow in her brow.

"King's Castle is worth too much simply to give it away," Faron said. "Unless you're anxious to get moved into town before winter comes."

"A few months won't make that much difference," Belinda replied. "Besides, we'd be making the man a thief if we accepted his offer."

The unspoken result of their decision not to sell King's Castle was a commitment to continue the improvements they had begun. But the changes they made now went further than simple repairs to put the ranch back into shape to sell. What Faron suggested to Belinda were modifications that would transform King's Castle into a viable, profitable ranching operation.

"Can we really afford to make these kinds of investments?" Belinda asked.

"They'll pay off in the long run," Faron said. It was as close as he could come to saying that he hoped there might be a "long run," without actually saying it. Because he feared saying it would put Belinda on the defensive. He wanted her to realize that they worked well together, that they made a good team, and that they could be happy making a life together on the ranch.

First she had to learn to trust him. He wasn't going to take the chance of pushing her too fast. So he had to keep his distance from her. Because if he took her to bed as often as he wanted to, it wouldn't take her long to figure out that he was playing for keeps. He wanted a chance to build good memories with her of life at King's Castle, to replace the bad ones that had made her want to flee the ranch.

Belinda searched out Faron's gray green eyes and was forced to drop her gaze or be singed by the need she saw there. Ever since their return from Texas there had been a palpable sexual tension between them. She kept waiting for Faron to act on it, to tease and taunt her as he had in the past. But he exercised a restraint that she wouldn't have believed possible.

She had no doubt that he desired her. It was there in the subtle electrical charge that passed between them whenever they brushed against each other. She saw it in the fierce light that came into his eyes as he gazed at her when he thought she wasn't looking. But she was confused by the signals he was sending.

He obviously wanted to be her lover. But he seemed to be waiting for her to make the first move. It was a novel idea to Belinda, who had never been allowed that option with Wayne. At the age of twenty-eight, she decided it was high time she tried her sexual wings.

She tried subtle things at first. One evening she was working at the computer station beside the rolltop desk while Faron sat in the swivel chair and examined the printout she had just made of feed projections for the winter. She stopped for a break and said, "My shoulders really ache. Could you rub them for me?"

The look in his eyes was priceless. He was a sinking man going down for the third time. "All right. I guess I could do that."

He dropped the printout on the desk, stood and crossed the few feet to where she was sitting. Belinda had her hair in a braid. "Would you mind undoing my braid first?" She saw the flush high on his cheekbones and felt a flutter of feminine satisfaction.

He took his time unraveling the braid, and when he was done his hand tunneled up underneath her long golden hair and massaged her scalp. Belinda's head rolled forward and she exposed her nape to his caresses. She could feel the strength of his hands where they worked to relax the muscles in her shoulders. She was feeling languorous, but there was a rising tension in her breasts and belly.

The moment came when he had to decide whether to continue what he was doing or escape the sensual torment caused by her request. She felt his lips on her nape, soft and slightly damp. A shiver chased down her spine as she felt his warm breath where he hovered over her.

Abruptly he stood up and said, "I need a cup of coffee. Can I get you one, too?"

She turned slightly toward him. He was standing and she was sitting and her eyes were level with the blunt ridge that stood out starkly against the fly of his jeans. She stared for a moment before she reached out a finger and traced the length of his arousal. Down. And then up.

She heard him swallow.

"Princess..."

She dropped her hand and said, "Yes, I'd like a cup of coffee. Thanks... Cowboy."

She turned back to the computer and began typing again. She could feel him standing there a moment longer, then heard his swift tread as he escaped the room and the sexual tension between them. Belinda couldn't help smiling when Faron was gone, pleased with the success of her plan. At this rate he wouldn't be able to hold out for long.

She was surprised the next morning over the breakfast table when he said, "What would you think about having a party to meet the neighbors?"

"That sounds like a wonderful idea," Maddy responded.

Belinda grimaced. She hadn't seen much of her neighbors since the disastrous party nearly six years ago when Wayne had publicly accused her of being a cold woman in bed. It was shortly after he had begun taking the heart medicine that had made him impotent. He had been drunk and had taken out his anger and frustration on her in the most publicly humiliating way possible. She wasn't sure she was ready to face any of those people ever again.

Maddy's enthusiasm was hard to stop. "I'll take care of the invitations," she said. "It's about time we had some music and laughter around here."

"But Maddy—" Belinda protested. "We're too busy to take time for a party."

"Nonsense. Rue and I will take care of everything. All you'll have to do is show up." She turned and beamed a smile at Faron. "I'm looking forward to showing off my grandson."

What could Belinda say to that?

Faron could see Belinda was less than enthusiastic about the party, but he didn't know why. But he decided that if she didn't want to confront her neighbors he wasn't going to force her into it, no matter what Maddy wanted. "We don't have to have a party, Princess. Just say the word and the plans will stop."

Belinda met Faron's concerned gaze, and if she hadn't already been in love with him she would have fallen for him then. He could have no idea why she didn't want to confront her neighbors. Yet he had been aware enough of her distress to respond to it, and in such a way that her needs and desires came before his own.

She smiled and reached out a hand to cover his where it lay on the table. "The party's a good idea. It's high time we said hello again to our neighbors."

Faron's hand turned under hers, and he lifted her hand and brought it to his lips. "Whatever you want, Princess."

What Belinda wanted in that moment was to go upstairs to bed. She blushed furiously at the thought, causing Maddy to chuckle and Faron's lids to droop lazily as he met the stark look of need in her eyes.

Abruptly he dropped her hand and stood. "Got work to do in the barn. See you later."

A moment later Maddy and Belinda were alone at the table.

"I'll be surprised if our neighbors accept an invitation to a party at King's Castle," Belinda said to Maddy. "I hope you know what you're doing." Belinda kept her eyes lowered to hide her pain as she admitted, "I'm afraid to face people after the insulting things Wayne said in public about our personal life."

"I don't think anyone ever blamed you for the way Wayne acted the last years of his life. It was plain to see that he wasn't well."

"I hope you're right," Belinda muttered. But she looked forward to the coming party with a feeling of dread.

The days before the party passed with unbelievable speed. Too soon Belinda found herself dressing with care for a party she had no desire to attend. When Faron knocked on her bedroom door to ask if she was ready to go downstairs she opened the door and said, "I can't go down there."

Faron stepped inside Belinda's bedroom and closed the door behind him. He took one look at the distress in her eyes and folded her into his arms. "What's the matter, Princess? Don't you know I'll protect you from the dragons?"

Just having him offer his support made her feel better. But Belinda knew these were dragons—of the past—that she had to face on her own. Yet there was no reason why she couldn't do so with Faron by her side. She stepped out of Faron's embrace and said, "I'm all right. I'm ready to go downstairs now."

But it suddenly dawned on both of them that they were alone in her bedroom with the door shut behind them. Faron grinned. "How about a kiss for luck?"

"Whose luck? Yours or mine?" Belinda quipped. Her apparent nonchalance was a sham. She felt breathless with excitement that was fed by the avid look in Faron's gray green eyes.

"Ours," Faron replied. "Have I told you how beautiful you look tonight?"

"No."

"You look absolutely breathtaking, Princess." He reached out and waited until she placed her hand in his. Then he drew her toward him until they were standing only inches apart. He cupped her jaw with his hand and raised her face to his. She no longer kept her lids lowered to hide her feelings from him. Blazing in her eyes was a need more than equal to his own. He lowered his mouth to hers and sipped of the nectar he found there.

His chest was tight with unspoken feelings. "If you need me tonight, I won't be far from your side."

He reached past her and opened the door, then took her arm and put it in the crook of his. "It's time to face your court, Princess. And if any of them dares to offer insult, it'll be off with his head!"

That brought a smile to Belinda's face that was still present when they reached the bottom of the circular staircase.

Most of their neighbors were already there, curious about Belinda and Faron and the reason for this party. Their looks were speculative as they eyed the widow and the roguish cowboy, but not unkind.

A young woman about Belinda's age, with brown hair and brown eyes and a vivid scar across one cheek, was the first to approach Belinda.

"Do you remember me?" she asked.

"Of course I do," Belinda replied. She remembered being appalled at the time that such a beautiful young woman should be so horribly scarred. She had been curious about what had happened, but had never gotten to know the woman well enough to ask. "Your name is Desiree."

The woman smiled and Belinda realized that the scar wasn't so visible after all. "That's right. I can't believe you remember it all these years."

"I remember it because you were so kind to me that night after..." Desiree Parrish had been the one who had finally stepped between Belinda and her husband.

"I only wish there had been more I could do to help," Desiree said. "I'm so glad you had this party. I've been hoping we could be friends."

This time it was Belinda who smiled. "I could use a friend or two."

"Maybe you'd like to come over next week and visit."

"Or you could come here," Belinda offered.

Desiree shook her head. "It's hard for me to find a babysitter. Would you mind?"

"Just name the day," Belinda said. "I'll be there."

The two women parted company knowing they had planted the seeds for a growing friendship.

By the end of the evening it was plain that everyone was more than willing to leave the past in the past.

True to his word, Faron stayed close by throughout Belinda's ordeal. She wasn't even aware that she was judging him, comparing him to his father.

She watched to see if he talked too loud and drank too much.

He didn't.

He nursed the same whiskey most of the evening, and while she occasionally heard his deep laughter, he was never boisterous.

She watched to see whether he told off-color jokes.

He didn't.

Whether he flirted with the ladies.

He did.

He had a way of making each woman feel special, while still making it clear that he intended their relationship to be strictly platonic.

Whether the neighbors respected him as a rancher and a businessman.

They did. Several times she caught him in discussions with the neighboring ranchers. He was as willing to take advice as he was to share his knowledge.

Whether he made snide or cruel remarks about their personal relationship.

He didn't. While he was never very far from her, he did nothing to indicate their relationship consisted of anything more than the legal connection between them.

But Belinda was mistaken if she thought her neighbors didn't see the attraction between the widow and the bastard son. What she would have discovered, if she had been watching, was that her neighbors were more than willing to accept such an alliance.

They already knew her to be a dedicated and caring rancher. Although Faron might be something of a rogue, he knew the ranching business. With a spread as large as King's Castle, it was important to have someone in authority who knew how to conserve the land.

Toward the end of the evening, Faron approached Belinda with another woman beside him. "Belinda, I think you know Pearl Teasdale. She was just telling me about a problem I thought you might be able to solve."

Pearl was a robust woman of forty-five, with gray hair she was proud of and calluses she had worked to earn. Her brown eyes were straightforward and her voice was slightly nasal from a deviated septum. "I was just telling Faron that Mrs. Webster had to resign as chairman of the Christmas pageant committee at the church when she found out she's expecting her third, only it's her third and fourth—twins, you see. So the doctor wants her to take it easy.

"Anyway, I was wondering if you might be willing to take the job as chairman and plan the pageant."

Belinda had been in the pageant as a child, and knew how much it meant to the children who participated. As a young woman, she hadn't been involved in the pageant, even though she had continued attending church.

"I—" She hesitated.

"Please say yes," Pearl urged. "We could really use the help. And Faron told me how much you love children."

"He did?" Belinda arched a brow. How could she argue with the truth? She would love spending time with the children. It was something Wayne had not allowed. "All right," she said. "I'll do it."

The smile on Pearl's face was blinding. "Wonderful!" She quickly called over several ladies, including Desiree, and they all began chattering about schedules and costumes.

Faron felt warm inside when he saw the way Belinda's face glowed with pleasure. There was light and laughter in her eyes. He frowned when he realized that he wasn't the only one admiring her. There was a bachelor or two among the assembled males, and Belinda was a beautiful, very eligible woman. He wanted to lay claim to her before some other man got ideas. However, he couldn't lay his claim in public when he hadn't made his intentions clear in private.

Faron was startled when he heard Maddy's quiet voice beside him.

"So, are you going to give that girl a child of her own?"

Faron's eyes hooded. His mouth flattened. "Don't interfere, Maddy. Everything in its own good time."

"Don't wait too long," Maddy warned.

Faron scowled. Maddy's warning reminded him too vividly of his fear that Belinda might finally decide she couldn't take a chance on marriage again. Maybe it was time to let Belinda Prescott know his true intentions. He stalked right over to her and easily maneuvered her away from the crowd of women.

"Excuse us, ladies. There's something I need to discuss with Belinda."

"What is it, Faron?"

He dragged her all the way into the kitchen before he stopped. He spied the pantry and hauled her inside the small room and closed the door behind them. The pantry was lit by a bare bulb, and they were surrounded by canned goods and preserves. He pressed her up against the closed door and kissed her with all the pent-up desire he had been saving for just such a moment.

"Faron, stop. What are you doing?"

"Kissing you. Loving you. It's what you want, isn't it?"

Belinda had been teasing him for weeks. It would be foolish to pretend she didn't want him now. She did. She kissed him back with zest and passion. She felt the zipper coming down on her dress and a moment later she was naked to the waist.

"You're not wearing a bra," he said as his hands reverently cupped her breasts. Belinda stepped out of the dress and laid it across several jars of stewed tomatoes.

"You're wearing a black garter belt," he said with a blissful sigh. He sounded a little shocked but pleased when he informed her, "Princess, you're not wearing any panties."

Belinda couldn't help the small giggle that escaped. "You sound like a teenage boy who just hit a home run with his girl," she teased.

"I feel like a kid in a candy store," he said. "I don't know what to taste first."

His mouth latched on to a nipple and he suckled strongly. Belinda arched toward him, but bit her lip to hold back the cry of ecstasy that sought voice.

There was a very real danger of discovery here, which only heightened her excitement.

Faron dropped to his knees and his mouth began a foray across her belly and down into the nest of blond curls below. His fingers and tongue indulged in a sensual feast that left her quivering. She would have fallen down if she hadn't been clutching his shoulders.

When he stood and kissed her again she could taste herself. The room smelled of sex and heat and desire. He didn't bother to remove his trousers, just unzipped them and shoved them down enough to free his aroused shaft. He lifted her and with one thrust sank deep inside her.

She wrapped her legs around his hips, her arms around his shoulders and buried her mouth against his throat. Her teeth closed on flesh, but she was unaware of the marks she was leaving as she felt herself driving toward the peak of ecstasy. His fingers bit into her, holding her tight as he thrust within her.

Their mouths merged, tongues thrusting, but they couldn't breathe and kiss at the same time. Belinda hid her face in Faron's shoulder as their bodies climaxed. He pressed his mouth to her cheek to cut off his guttural cry of pleasure.

They stood there for scant moments panting, until Belinda's legs dropped down to support her.

She heard Faron's chuckle and smiled. "You're a crazy man, Cowboy," she said huskily.

"Then may I never be sane," he answered in an equally throaty voice.

To their chagrin and amusement there was a quiet knock at the pantry door. "You might want to rejoin your guests to bid them good night," Maddy said.

"We'll be there in a minute, Maddy," Faron answered her.

Belinda felt the door opening behind her. "Wait—"

A hand slipped inside bearing a damp towel. "I thought you might need this."

The door closed, and they heard Maddy walking away.

They took one look at each other and burst out laughing. Belinda put a hand on Faron's mouth. "Shh. We'll be caught."

He took the towel and put it to good use on her and himself. Belinda stepped into her dress and turned so he could zip her up. "Do you suppose they'll know what we've been doing?"

Belinda's hair had been left down tonight, but it looked considerably more windblown than when they had entered the pantry. Faron did his best to smooth it. Then he turned her around to face him, took one look at the sparkle in her eye and said, "They'd have to be blind not to know."

Belinda caught a glimpse of the satisfied smile on Faron's face and pursed her lips. "It might help if you wipe that grin off your face."

He shook his head. "Uh uh. No can do. Feels too good."

Belinda gave up and joined him. "I suppose it does."

They returned to the party at intervals as though they had long ago gone their separate ways to do errands that had only just been completed. If their neighbors suspected what Belinda and Faron had been doing while they were gone, they were too polite to say anything about it.

Over the weeks and months that followed, Faron and Belinda were seen often in each other's company. At church. At the feed store in Casper. Riding the borders of King's Castle. At the Grange dances. Though no words had been spoken between them to declare it so, they were a couple.

Belinda radiated a new self-confidence. She worked with several ladies who had taken part in the Christmas pageant in the past to make sure that she didn't forget anything. And she loved working with the children. They were delightful. Open and loving and honest. She felt an undeniable yearning—which she fought—for a child of her own.

She made love to Faron as often as she could and in as many ways and places as they could devise. She couldn't help feeling that she was living on borrowed time. That the magical fairy tale they had created simply couldn't last. She was too happy, and she couldn't help feeling that there had to be a villain somewhere—every fairy tale had one—who would strip away her happiness.

As Christmas approached, she asked Faron to save some time to help her set up the tree. They decided to do it the third Saturday afternoon in December.

The boxes of Christmas decorations were kept in a room on the third floor of The Castle. Faron hadn't been up there before, and he was amazed at the history he saw in the items stored there.

"A lot of families must have lived in this house over the years," he said. He picked up a *McGuffey's Reader* and paged through it. There was a handmade wooden wagon and a rocking horse that would have been about the right size for a child of four or five.

Belinda picked up a reticule, a purse once carried by a pioneer woman, and donned a silk bonnet. "What do you think? Am I ready for a trip into town?"

"You look ready for a kiss." He lowered his mouth to hers and their lips met in the tenderest of kisses. "Belinda, don't you want to be a part of this? To preserve King's Castle for future generations?"

"I—I thought that's what we were doing."

Faron's voice was harsh when he responded, "Are we? Or are we just fooling ourselves, playing games until a buyer comes along and snatches all this out from under us?"

"That's not fair, Cowboy," Belinda retorted in a heated voice. "If anybody's playing games here, it's you. What is it you want from me?"

Maddy's voice filtered up the stairs. "Faron? Belinda? Are you up there? There's someone here to see you."

"We'll talk about this tonight," Faron said. He didn't give Belinda a chance to argue, just grabbed her hand and headed down the stairs.

When they arrived downstairs they found a man slightly older than Faron waiting for them. He had chestnut brown hair and cold blue eyes. He was about Faron's height, but heavier in build, with a bigger chest and shoulders. He was wearing faded jeans and a ragged shirt and his boots hadn't seen polish in a month of Sundays.

"Hello," he said, extending his hand to Faron. "I'm Carter Prescott. Your brother. I'm here to take this place off your hands."

Ten

"**I** should have known that Wayne Prescott had more than one bastard son," Faron said bitterly.

"I'm not a bastard," Carter said in a frosty voice. "Wayne Prescott was married to my mother."

Both Faron and Belinda turned to Madelyn for confirmation. She nodded slowly. "It's true. Wayne was married once, a long time ago. The marriage ended in divorce, but as far as I know there were no children."

Carter smiled cynically. "I was conceived after the divorce papers had been filed and born shortly before the divorce was final. There was no love lost between my mother and Wayne Prescott. She didn't see any reason to let him know he had a son.''

"Why have you waited until now to come forward?" Faron asked.

"I wouldn't have said anything even now, except I want this place and I thought I'd have a better chance of getting it as a Prescott."

Faron forked all ten fingers through his hair. "Damn. I'm not sure what the legalities are—whether you're entitled to a portion of King's Castle under the will or not."

"I don't give a damn about any inheritance I might be entitled to."

Faron frowned. "Then why are you here?"

"I want to buy King's Castle."

Faron looked skeptically at the man standing in front of him. Carter Prescott didn't look like someone who had the kind of money it was going to take to buy a ranch the size of King's Castle. "Do you have that kind of cash?"

Carter's lips curled into a wry smile. "In the divorce my mother took Wayne Prescott for half of everything he owned. Over the years I've made a few investments." He shrugged apologetically. "I'm rich as sin."

Faron turned stunned eyes on Belinda.

"I'm willing to pay you what the place is worth," Carter said. "Money is no object. Name your price. I'm just looking for some roots, and I think I might find them here."

Faron couldn't argue with that sentiment. He had felt it himself. But this was *his* place. Carter Prescott would have to find his roots somewhere else!

"I think Belinda and I need to have a discussion in private. Would you mind giving us some time alone?" Faron said.

"Sure." Carter turned to Madelyn and took off his hat to introduce himself. "If I'm not mistaken, you're my grandmother."

"I am," Madelyn said. There was a distinct chill in her voice that surprised Faron. "I never liked your mother," Madelyn said to Carter.

Carter smiled ruefully. "Not many people did, ma'am."

That defrosted a little of Madelyn's ice, but she couldn't embrace this new-found grandson when she believed he was determined to ruin the happiness of the other.

"I could use a cup of coffee," Carter said.

"Come with me." Madelyn turned and marched toward the kitchen without looking back.

Carter settled his Stetson on his head and followed resolutely after her.

Of all the forms the villain in Belinda's fairy tale had taken, it was never that of a handsome young man. "I can't believe this is happening," she said.

"It's happening," Faron said. "Let's go into the study where we can sit down and talk."

Belinda was too nervous to sit down. Once Faron was settled in the swivel chair in front of the desk, she jumped up and began pacing.

"With the money from the sale of King's Castle, you and Maddy will both have the security you wanted," Faron began.

Belinda looked at him with stricken eyes. That wasn't what she wanted to hear from Faron. She wanted to hear that he loved her and wanted to marry her and that together they would spend their lives making King's Castle what it once was.

But she couldn't force him to stay if he wanted to go. And with Hawk's Way calling to him, how could she ever have hoped he might want to stay?

"I suppose it makes sense to accept Carter's offer," she said tentatively.

"Is that what you really want to do?" Faron asked.

"I'm willing to go along with whatever you want to do," Belinda countered, her eyes lowered to hide the grief she felt at the loss that was to come. "So I guess we sell."

Faron's tone was grim, "If that's what you want to do, then that's what we'll do." He kept his eyes lowered to the hands fisted in his lap.

Neither one of them realized they were sacrificing what they most wanted in deference to the needs and wants of the other.

"Do you want to tell him our decision now?" Faron asked.

"Not yet!" Belinda didn't know why she felt so frantic, only that she did. "Let's wait until after the pageant tonight."

"Postponing the inevitable isn't going to change it," Faron warned.

"I know. Please, Faron. Just wait until after the pageant." She could keep her fairy tale alive for a few more hours. It wasn't over yet, and she didn't plan to give up her dream until she absolutely had to.

Faron didn't know what else to say. "We'd better finish getting that tree up. You've got to be at the church early tonight to set up for the Christmas pageant."

When Faron and Belinda entered the kitchen, Madelyn and Carter were engaged in a rousing argument.

"What's going on here?" Faron asked.

"I was just trying to talk Carter into attending the Christmas pageant tonight. Without much success, I might add."

"Oh, please come," Belinda said. "It's so moving."

"That's what I'm afraid of," Carter muttered. "I don't care much for that sort of thing."

"But it's Christmas," Belinda said. "Everyone loves Christmas."

Faron took one look at Carter's face and realized his stepbrother was the exception. "You don't have to come if you'd rather not."

Madelyn wasn't about to let Carter off that easily. "I'd appreciate the chance to show off *both* my grandsons. Surely you won't deny me that."

"All right, Maddy," Carter said. But it was plain his heart wasn't in it.

"The children have worked so hard. I know you'll enjoy it," Belinda said. "They do a wonderful job."

The more Belinda said about children, the more rigid Carter's face got, until she realized she was only making it worse by going on and on. She didn't know what Carter Prescott had against children and Christmas, but it was clear his opinions were long-standing. Nothing she said was going to change them.

In the awkward silence that ensued Carter said, "By the way, did you make a decision about selling King's Castle?"

Belinda and Faron exchanged an uneasy glance.

"We want to think about it a little while longer," Faron said.

"Goodness. This is no time to be worrying about business," Madelyn interjected. "Look at the time. If we don't get busy, we'll be late getting to the pageant."

Belinda was so excited, she and Faron left early for church. Carter promised to follow later with Madelyn. It had begun snowing, and while Belinda was glad for the hope of a white Christmas, she was worried that the threat of a bad storm might keep some families away from the pageant. She was proved wrong when she arrived at the church and saw the pews were already beginning to fill.

She rushed around setting robes in place on shoulders, making sure the shepherds had their staffs and the angels had their halos. At the last moment there was some confusion about whether it was all right to use a female doll to represent the baby Jesus. Belinda did some fast talking and got the youngster playing Joseph to agree to the deception.

Belinda watched the program from the sidelines, nestled in the curve of Faron's arm. "The children are so precious," she whispered. Unspoken was the wish for some of her own.

Belinda watched Faron watching the children and saw his eyes soften with tenderness as a six-year-old Mary nestled a baby doll Jesus in her arms. She watched them light with laughter as an eight-year-old shepherd scattered live sheep down the aisle of the church. And watched them glow with what she would have sworn was love as he turned to her and squeezed her hand while they sang "Silent Night."

When the pageant was over and all the children had been divested of their costumes and bundled into coats, Belinda and Faron looked for Carter and Madelyn. All they found was Maddy.

"Carter left," Madelyn said. "He said he would meet us back at the house."

"But why?" Belinda asked.

"I think it was too hard for him to stay any longer," Madelyn said mysteriously. Belinda never could get any more of an explanation from Madelyn all the way home. At last Belinda realized there must be a lot of people like herself and Carter who had pasts they would rather forget. She felt a little guilty for forcing Carter into a situation where he had been forced to confront demons he might rather have left resting in their dens.

When they got back to The Castle, they found Carter settled in front of the fireplace with a brandy. There was no sign either in his face or his greeting that suggested a reason for why he had left the church.

"If you're comfortable, Carter, I think we'll just leave you here for a while. Belinda and I need to talk privately with Maddy," Faron said.

"I'll be fine," Carter said. "Don't worry about me."

As Faron and Belinda ushered Madelyn into the study, she demanded to know what was going on. Faron refused to say anything until Madelyn was seated in the swivel chair in front of the rolltop desk.

"Why all this hush-hush secretive business?" Madelyn demanded.

"Belinda and I wanted you to hear that we've decided to sell King's Castle before I inform Carter about the deal."

"What!" Madelyn rose with a vigor that denied her age and her ailing heart.

It was apparent from her ruddy complexion and the outrage in her voice that even though Faron and Belinda were willing to be so foolish as to give up their dreams, Madelyn was not.

"I absolutely refuse to leave this house!" she said. It was more of a shriek, actually.

Faron and Belinda stared at the agitated woman who stood across from them, her hands twisting a lace handkerchief. Madelyn was having trouble catching her breath.

"Please sit down, Maddy." Faron was seriously concerned that she might make herself sick. He tried to get her back into the swivel chair.

Madelyn eluded him and marched around to stand beside the desk with her back to the wall. "Don't coddle me! I won't sit down until I hear from your own lips, Belinda, that you would even consider something as horrendous as selling this house out from under me!"

"But Madelyn, I thought you understood that was why Faron and I were making all these improvements," Belinda said.

"Well, I didn't understand!" Madelyn said in an imperious voice. She turned her irate gaze on Faron. "As for you, young man, I'm gravely disappointed in you."

Faron felt the heat on his cheekbones and wasn't sure whether he was feeling shame, embarrassment or anger. Actually, it was a combination of all three. "What is it you're most disappointed by, Maddy? The fact that I would court your son's wife in front of your nose? Or the fact that I'm willing to make Belinda happy at your expense?"

"You young idiot! Don't you see that selling King's Castle isn't going to make anyone happy? Least of all Belinda!"

"You're wrong. Belinda told me months ago that she wants to live in town. She just got through telling me she wants to sell this place."

"Foolish man! Belinda was willing to move into town to take care of me. She would never leave King's Castle if you decided to stay here with her. Ask her!"

Faron leapt up from his chair and turned to face Belinda. "Is that true, Belinda? Would you stay at King's Castle if I stayed here with you?"

"Since that isn't going to happen—"

Faron grabbed Belinda by the shoulders and shook her. "Answer the damned question!"

"Yes! I'd never leave this place if you were here with me. But Faron, that isn't possible, don't you see?"

"Why not?"

"Do you mean to say you'd be willing to leave Hawk's Way? That you'd be willing to spend the rest of your life in Wyoming?"

"I'd move to hell and set up housekeeping if you were there with me. I love you, Princess."

Belinda stood stunned. "Why didn't you ever tell me so?"

Faron shrugged sheepishly. "I didn't want to scare you away. What I want, Princess, what I've wanted for what seems a very long time, is to marry you and work this ranch and raise children here with you."

Belinda thought of the risk involved in committing herself to another man. What she discovered was that her love for Faron, and his love for her, took all the fear out of taking such a risk. Faron wanted only to make her happy, just as she wanted to please him.

"If that was a proposal," she said at last, "I accept."

Faron threw his arms around Belinda and hugged her so tightly she squeaked.

"Don't squeeze the girl to death," Madelyn chided.

Faron reached out and included Maddy in the hug. "You conniving old woman. I don't know what you're complaining about. You got exactly what you wanted."

Madelyn grinned and chortled. "I suppose I did at that. Now. What are we going to do about that young man in the parlor?"

"We have to invite him to stay for Christmas," Belinda said. "We can't send him off alone."

Madelyn's eyes narrowed speculatively. "No, we can't do that, can we?"

"You're not matchmaking again, are you Madelyn?" Belinda asked when she spied the look in her mother-in-law's eyes.

"Who? Me, dear? What makes you think that? However, Carter did mention while we were having coffee in the kitchen that he owns a ski resort in Vermont. It's located in a town not far from where Fiona runs her bed and breakfast. Two relatives should get to know each other, don't you think?"

"Carter's not related in the least to Fiona!" Belinda protested.

"No, they're not related, are they?" Madelyn murmured. "How fortunate. But I do foresee a slight problem."

Belinda knew she shouldn't ask, but did anyway. "What problem?"

"Carter doesn't like cats."

"How did you find that out?" Faron asked, amazed at how much information Madelyn had pried from her newest grandson in the little time they'd had together. "About Carter and cats?"

"Oh, we were discussing conservation. Carter's working to save the mountain lion, even though he doesn't like cats. I don't suppose Fiona would be willing to give up Tut..."

"Madelyn—"

Belinda's warning was lost as Madelyn headed for the parlor. "I'll just go get Carter and send him in here so you can give him the bad news."

When she was gone Belinda looked up at Faron and shook her head. "I don't think there's any help for it. I suppose I'll have to call Fiona and warn her what's coming."

Faron grinned. "What, and spoil all Maddy's fun? From what I know of your sister, Fiona can take care of herself."

"At least it looks like our fairy tale is going to end happily ever after," Belinda said as she gazed up at Faron with adoring eyes.

"What do you want for Christmas, Princess?"

"A baby."

"You've got it. But I think I'll go ahead and give you the gift I had planned." Faron opened the top right hand desk drawer and reached into the back of it. He pulled out a small velvet box and opened it. "This is for you, Princess."

Inside was a topaz surrounded by baguette diamonds. "It's the closest thing I could find to the daisies we picked that first day we spent together." He took the ring from the box and placed it on her finger. "Now you'll always be wearing flowers, Princess."

Tears blurred Belinda's vision. "It's beautiful. Thanks, Cowboy."

All things considered, Carter Prescott took the news that King's Castle had been taken off the market pretty well. "You know I could go to court and challenge the will," he pointed out. "I could tie up your assets so you'd have a hell of a time making ends meet.''

"You could," Faron said, a muscle ticking in his jaw. ''But I'd fight you every step of the way. And I have some considerable assets at my disposal.''

Carter measured Faron's determination and apparently decided Faron meant what he said. Carter smiled wistfully. "I envy you, brother. Guess I'll have to keep looking for those roots.''

"I wish you luck finding them," Faron said. ''You'll always be welcome here. In fact, we'd be pleased to have you join us for Christmas.''

Carter shook his head. "I don't think so. I don't want to intrude. In fact, I'll be leaving tonight.''

"So soon?" Belinda asked. "I know Madelyn would like to spend more time with you.''

Carter shook his head. "If I stay here much longer I might get to liking this place too much.'' He reached out his hand to Faron. "Goodbye, Faron. It was a pleasure meeting you.''

Faron shook his stepbrother's hand. "I wish we had more time to get to know each other.''

"Maybe I'll be back this way again sometime.''

Faron and Belinda walked Carter to the parlor where they found Madelyn. She was distressed that her grandson had chosen to leave so soon, but didn't try to change his mind.

Carter hugged his grandmother. "I'm glad I met you, Maddy. I'll see you again sometime.'' But the way he said it didn't sound like he thought it would be anytime soon.

"Maybe sooner than you think," Madelyn said with a smug smile.

Belinda shook her head. Once Madelyn got an idea in her head it was hard to get it out. Somehow the old woman had gotten her mind set on matching Carter and Fiona. Belinda decided the best thing to do was to stand back and watch the fur fly. Considering how Carter felt about cats, that was a definite possibility when he met up with Tut.

The three of them stood at the door and waved as Carter drove away. It didn't take long for his pickup to disappear in the flurries of snow.

"Now that our company's gone, I think I'll go to bed," Madelyn announced. "I'm feeling a little tired tonight."

Faron and Belinda looked at each other anxiously.

"Are you all right, Maddy?" Faron asked.

Madelyn grinned. "Now don't you worry about me. I plan to be around long enough to dandle a couple of great-grandchildren on my knee. I just thought I'd leave you two alone so you could get started." Madelyn winked, then turned and headed up the stairs.

Faron and Belinda stood stunned for a second before they burst out laughing.

"I can take a hint," Faron said. He lifted Belinda into his arms and headed for the parlor. He set her down on the rug in front of the fireplace and joined her there. The only light in the room came from the fire and the colored bulbs on the Christmas tree.

They didn't speak, just sat and held each other, listening to the fire crackle and the wind howl as it blew snow against the house. The aroma of spruce pervaded the room, bringing the vast reaches of King's Castle inside for Christmas.

Faron kissed Belinda's cheek, and she snuggled back into his arms. "It's nice holding you like this," he said.

"It's nice being held."

"Would you like to get married on Christmas Day?"

"That would be nice," Belinda said. "Maybe we could get your family and mine both to come here for the occasion."

"I suspect we might be able to talk them into it."

"I love you, Faron."

He smiled. "You know, that's the first time you've said that to me."

"Is it, really? I've thought it a thousand times."

"I hope you'll keep on saying it."

"I love you. Love you. Love you." She punctuated each pronouncement with a kiss.

Faron slowly lowered Belinda to the rug in front of the fireplace. "Your eyes are lit up like the Christmas tree," he said.

"I can't tell you how happy I feel. Maybe I can show you."

She slowly began covering his face with kisses while her hands roamed his body seeking out the places she had learned would bring him the most pleasure.

"Let's make our baby here, now," she murmured. "Love me, Cowboy."

Faron didn't need more invitation than that. They wasted no time undressing each other, and soon their bodies lay entwined like two golden stems in the firelight. Faron spread Belinda's legs with his knees and settled himself in the cradle of her thighs.

"How many children shall we have?" he murmured as he kissed his way up her throat toward her ear.

"At least a boy and a girl."

He grinned. "I knew a family that had six girls before they got a boy."

Belinda flushed. "I think I could be happy with just girls. Or just boys."

Faron's hand slipped down past her belly to the nest of curls below. She was already wet, and he didn't wait, just slid himself inside her. Then he lay there, waiting to see how long he could stand the pleasure before he had to move.

Meanwhile, Belinda was busy playing with the curls on his chest. She found a male nipple and laved it with her tongue. Faron jerked, and the friction of their bodies moving together wrought a soft cry of pleasure from Belinda's throat.

"Don't move," Faron begged. "I'm trying an experiment here."

Belinda lifted her hips and Faron groaned.

"What kind of experiment?" she asked.

"I wanted to see how long we could just lie here joined together like this."

Belinda grinned like a cat with a bowl of cream. "Not long, Cowboy."

She shifted again and Faron fought back a guttural sound in his throat. "Princess, I'm serious about this."

"So am I." Belinda reached down between their two bodies and touched him where they were joined. Her hand slid down and gently cupped the sac below.

Faron wasn't able to stay still under her onslaught. "All right, if that's the way you want to play, I'm game."

He reached down between them and found the heart of her desire. In moments his caresses had her undulating with pleasure.

"What do you say, Cowboy? Ready to cry uncle?"

"Not until you do, Princess," Faron replied.

Faron latched onto a nipple and suckled hard.

"That's cheating," Belinda rasped.

Faron was too busy to answer. Belinda threaded her hands in his hair and urged his mouth up to hers. "I want to be your woman, Cowboy. I want to have your baby."

Faron answered, "I love you, Princess. I want to make love with you tonight and tomorrow and the rest of our lives."

Their loving was like a prayer, a litany to happily ever after. As their bodies succumbed to the demands each made upon the other, their souls entwined once and for always.

With the woman he loved in his arms, Faron said a prayer that the weather would hold good over the winter so they would have enough feed to manage without buying more. And that his new wife would present him with a daughter in the fall, along about harvest time.

Belinda said a prayer that she would be a good and loving wife, and that she would present her new husband with a son in the fall, along about harvest time.

And just like in a fairy tale, both their prayers were answered.

*   *   *   *   *

SILHOUETTE® Desire®

HAWK'S WAY

HAWK'S WAY—where the Whitelaws of Texas run free till passion brands their hearts. A hot new series from Joan Johnston!

Look for the first of a long line of Texan adventures, beginning in April with THE RANCHER AND THE RUNAWAY BRIDE (D #779), as Tate Whitelaw battles her bossy brothers—and a sexy rancher.

Next, in May, Faron Whitelaw meets his match in THE COWBOY AND THE PRINCESS (D #785).

Finally, in June, Garth Whitelaw shows you just how hot the summer can get in THE WRANGLER AND THE RICH GIRL (D #791).

Join the Whitelaws as they saunter about HAWK'S WAY looking for their perfect mates . . . only from Silhouette Desire!

Take 4 bestselling love stories FREE

Plus get a FREE surprise gift!

Special Limited-time Offer

Mail to Harlequin Reader Service®

3010 Walden Avenue
P.O. Box 1867
Buffalo, N.Y. 14269-1867

YES! Please send me 4 free Silhouette Desire® novels and my free surprise gift. Then send me 6 brand-new novels every month, which I will receive months before they appear in bookstores. Bill me at the low price of $2.24* each plus 25¢ delivery and applicable sales tax, if any.* I understand that accepting the books and gift places me under no obligation ever to buy any books. I can always return a shipment and cancel at any time. Even if I never buy another book from Silhouette, the 4 free books and the surprise gift are mine to keep forever.

225 BPA AJCJ

Name	(PLEASE PRINT)	
Address	Apt. No.	
City	State	Zip

This offer is limited to one order per household and not valid to present Silhouette Desire® subscribers.
*Terms and prices are subject to change without notice. Sales tax applicable in N.Y.

UDES-93

©1990 Harlequin Enterprises Limited